Sadie slit open the back of the envelope and withdrew the contents.

A Polaroid fell face-down on the counter. She turned over the picture, and gasped. A man with lifeless eyes stared into the camera. She dropped the photograph and reached for the newspaper clipping.

Not just a clipping—an obituary with today's date. She stared at the man's grainy picture in the paper, then grabbed the Polaroid and compared the photographs.

Same man!

Icy fingers trailed her back.

She set the clipping on the counter and unfolded the piece of paper. Her hands trembled so badly, she almost couldn't read the letter.

Sadie pressed her lips together, holding her breath as she read.

> YOUR BROTHER WILL BE NEXT IF YOU DON'T DO EXACTLY AS YOU ARE TOLD. INSTRUCTIONS TO FOLLOW SOON. DO NOT NOTIFY THE POLICE. WAIT TO HEAR FROM US.

The paper drifted from her slack fingers.

Dear Lord, help me.

Books by Robin Caroll

Love Inspired Suspense

Bayou Justice
Bayou Corruption
Bayou Judgment
Bayou Paradox
Bayou Betrayal
Framed!
Blackmail

ROBIN CAROLL

Born and raised in Louisiana, Robin Caroll is Southern to a fault. Her passion has always been to tell stories to entertain others. When she isn't writing, Robin spends time with her husband of nineteen years, her three beautiful daughters and their four character-filled pets at home—in the South, where else? An avid reader herself, Robin loves hearing from and chatting with other readers. Although her favorite genre to read is mystery/suspense, of course, she'll read just about any good story. Except historicals! To learn more about this author of Deep South mysteries of suspense to inspire your heart, visit Robin's Web site at www.robincaroll.com.

ROBIN CAROLL
BLACKMAIL

Steeple
Hill®

Published by Steeple Hill Books™

STEEPLE HILL BOOKS

Steeple
Hill®

Recycling programs
for this product may
not exist in your area.

ISBN-13: 978-0-373-44344-4

BLACKMAIL

www.SteepleHill.com

Printed in U.S.A.

Blessed is he who has regard for the weak;
the Lord delivers him in times of trouble.
—*Psalms* 41:1

Speak up and judge fairly; defend the rights
of the poor and needy.
—*Proverbs* 31:9

To Brandon and Rachel…
I'm so proud to be your aunt!

Acknowledgments

My most heartfelt gratitude to…

Amazing editors and friends, Krista Stroever and
Elizabeth Mazer, who energize me with their enthusiasm.

"Super Agent" Kelly Mortimer. Love ya!

Mentor and dear friend, Colleen Coble, who continues to
help me learn and grow in this industry.

Camy, Cara, Cheryl, Dineen, Heather, Lisa, Pammer,
Ronie, Trace and Wanda, for input and support.
Love y'all.

The employees of the State of Louisiana's Department of
Natural Resource, Office of Oil and Gas Conservation,
but especially to my sister, Cindy Pittman, and the
brilliant Charlie Boyd, who answered my vast and tiring
questions about the oil industry. Any errors in the way of
the oil business are my own, twisted to best work in my
fictional story.

My family for continued encouragement: Mom, Papa,
Bek, Krystina, BB, Robert, Bubba, Lisa, Bill and
Connie, and all the rest!

Emily, Remington and Isabella—
you are my greatest inspirations.

Case—without your love, support and encouragement,
I couldn't do this.

All glory to my Lord and Savior, Jesus Christ.

ONE

Four hours, twenty-eight minutes of driving, only to sit and cool her heels.

Sadie Thompson had left Lagniappe, Louisiana, at three-thirty this hot and humid July morning to make sure she wouldn't be late to pick up her half brother Caleb at eight, sharp. Which meant she'd set her alarm for three. Now she stood in the main room of the Terrebonne Parish Juvenile Detention Center, pacing as she waited for them to process Caleb out of the system.

Her soles squeaked against the buffed floor. What would he be like after all these years of living with his father? No telling what lies that man, an oil field worker, had filled Caleb's mind with. Of course, she shouldn't speak ill of the dead, but she'd never liked Caleb's father. But she'd come this far and she'd see this through. Besides, she wouldn't allow what happened to Uncle Joe to happen to Caleb. Not if she could help it.

Who knew, maybe they could build a real brother–sister relationship. It wasn't as if she had anyone else—she had no other living relatives. Didn't even have any friends aside from her pastor.

She'd spent hours last night readying her guest room for her brother. Cleared out all the floral-printed curtains and comforter, replacing them with a navy blue set. Maybe it was silly because he'd be her charge only for the few months until his eighteenth birthday, but Sadie wanted to make the effort. Make Caleb feel welcome. She'd made sure her kitchen was well-stocked. Wasn't it a fact that teenage boys had bottomless pits for stomachs?

Vibrations ran along her hip. Sadie jerked her cell from the belt clip and pushed it open. "Hello."

"Another facility's been sabotaged. One of the new ones. The rednecks are now picketing outside the office, claiming that if we hadn't laid them off, this wouldn't be happening. Deacon's blowing a gasket and asking for you." Georgia, Sadie's assistant public relations representative, sounded flustered. And Georgia Maldon never got flustered. "On top of that, those fishermen are making a stink again. They're getting more vocal."

Great. Just par for a Monday. Why did the bottom have to fall out today of all days? "Look, I can't come in. You'll just have to deal with Deacon."

Deacon Wynn, owner and president of Vermilion Oil. Her boss. Shrewd and ruthless. And very accustomed to having people jump when he spoke.

"Sadie, don't do this to me." Georgia's voice dropped to a whisper. "He's ballistic. Second facility sabotaged within a month, and the media's all over it. Fifty-eight wells produced into this facility. He says we're losing business right and left and you'd better do damage control. Or else."

She glanced at her watch—barely eight forty-five. How much longer would she be left waiting? How much paperwork could it take to release someone from prison? Wait, this wasn't prison, this was a juvenile detention center. Wasn't that what the court representative had harped over and over? Caleb had been brought in for downloading pirated DVDs and music off the Internet, of all things. According to the representatives, the judge had sentenced him to incarceration for sixty days only to teach Caleb a lesson to deter his misguided life direction.

"Sadie, please." Georgia's voice cracked.

Running a hand over her hair, Sadie felt as if she were being pulled in two different directions. Right now, she couldn't leave. "I can't help it. I'm out of town right now and can't make it in."

Stave Deacon off by telling him I'll get a press release out to the media today." If she could get in touch with her contact at the *Lagniappe Gazette,* she could head off the rumors against the company. She knew better than most how much the locals loved to wag their tongues. Hadn't she been trying to live down her own past reputation? "Set up an appointment with the fishermen for later this week. I'll try to smooth over their concerns. And call security and see if they can do anything about the picketing. If those guys are on our property, we can have them removed."

"Deacon's going to want to see you, Sadie. He needs to hear directly from you that this is under control."

If it wasn't one thing, it was another. Her nerves bunched into tightly coiled springs as she stared at the door the guard had told her Caleb would exit from. She gripped the cell tighter. "Tell Deacon I'll work out an angle and call him later. Bye." She closed the phone and slid it back onto her hip, dropping into one of the plastic chairs as she did so.

Sadie loved working as the public relations officer for Vermilion Oil. Loved working angles. But over the last two weeks, with sabotages…well, the situation had become a scramble for damage control. Now she was about to add another layer of stress to her life—custody of her brother. Had she lost her ever-loving mind?

She tried to remember what Caleb had been like as a child. It'd been too many years to count since they'd lived under the same roof. Sullen, she remembered that much about him, but when he smiled…oh, my, when he smiled, he could melt your heart. But she hadn't seen Caleb in the seven years since their mother's funeral, and if memory served her correct, it hadn't exactly been a warm and fuzzy reunion. More like an icy reception.

He'd grown tall and lanky, like his father, whom Sadie had never liked. Caleb had long, dark, greasy-looking hair, but also had been blessed with their mother's eyes, glimmering with proof that he could be capable of kindness and gentleness.

What was she supposed to do with a half brother she didn't even know? Especially one who'd been incarcerated?

Sadie crossed her legs and reviewed the paperwork the

juvenile system had provided her. As if she hadn't read it four times already.

She'd have to take Caleb directly to the parole office upon his release. They would meet with his assigned parole officer, one Jon Garrison.

Parole offices, incidents which were in violation of parole and would result in immediate revocation of Caleb's release and sessions with summer school counselors to ensure her brother would integrate back into the public school system without difficulty...all foreign to her before today. Now, these issues would become a part of her daily life.

But everyone deserved a second chance. She knew that better than most. Hadn't she been busy for the last year trying to prove to the people of Lagniappe she was no longer the woman with questionable morals?

The door creaked open next to the guard's post. Sadie shot to her feet, nervous energy tightening her muscles. Caleb dwarfed the guard beside him. Her brother stood over six feet tall, quite a difference from seven years ago. The gray sweatpants hung off his lean frame. His hair was different—short, almost trimmed into a buzz. That probably wasn't a choice, but a requirement of the detention center policy. Acne pocked his freshly shaven face, a reminder that despite his size, he was still a minor.

Probably with a little boy's heart.

She rushed forward, unsure whether to hug him. She sucked her bottom lip and halted, waiting for him to make the first move.

He lifted his bowed head. His stare met hers.

Cold. Unfriendly. Resentful.

She swallowed back the hope. "Caleb." She struggled to smile.

The guard handed him a black trash bag. "Stay outta trouble, Caleb."

Again, her sullen brother didn't reply. He strutted toward the front doors, attitude seeping from his every movement.

The man touched Sadie's shoulder. "Better keep up with

him." He glanced at Caleb's retreating back. "Best of luck, lady. You're gonna need it."

Oh, Father, please help me.

"Here's a new one for you."

Jon Garrison glanced up from the mountain of paperwork piled on the desk in front of him. He glared at the young clerk assigned to his parole office. "You're not serious." He leaned back in his chair and ran a hand over his face.

"Sorry, boss. I'm just the messenger." Lisa passed him a file, grinning.

He set the folder on top of his stack. It nearly toppled to the floor. Typical Monday chaos.

She chuckled, enjoying his angst way too much.

"Don't they realize I'm only one person? I can't handle this type of caseload."

"Request another parole officer be assigned to the office."

If it were only that easy. "Like that will happen. Haven't you heard budget cuts have caused several offices to close? Why do you think I moved here?"

"Because you got smart and wanted to live south of the Mason-Dixon line?" Her smile matched her comment—tongue-in-cheek.

"Cute." Days like this, Jon wished he was back in Nebraska, where there were four seasons and snow wasn't something just seen on Christmas cards. The weather here was crazy. He'd been here since February and had yet to be able to differentiate between seasons except for warm, hot and humid. And that fourth season? Warm, hot and humid all blended together.

"Seriously, Jon, if there are too many cases, just call the state office. If no one complains about the overload in each office, they'll never do anything about it." She shrugged. "I'm gonna grab a burger for lunch. Want one?"

Another greasy, fried meal? Jon's stomach turned. Then rumbled. "Nope. I'm going to go eat a real meal." He grabbed the new file and his windbreaker. "But it'll be a working lunch."

"Want some company?"

The last thing he wanted, or needed, was to have his assistant getting the wrong idea. Not that the perky redhead wasn't attractive; she was. But he wasn't interested, and a too-comfortable relationship between coworkers wasn't a smart idea. That would just be an invitation for a sticky situation, or a sexual harassment suit, neither of which sounded the least bit appealing.

"I think I'm just going to bury my head in this latest file and see what I can get set up. Won't be very good company."

"See you in an hour, then." She rushed from the doorway.

The possibility of miscommunication between them was a complication he couldn't handle right now. Not on top of an already full caseload, with more arriving daily. What had he let himself in for, moving here? He'd believed he could help people, make a difference. Wasn't that what his supervisor had said? When the Nebraska county he'd resided in fell victim to the dreaded budget cuts, the move had sounded like a good idea. But now…

Jon allowed enough time for Lisa to get free of the parking lot before he walked to his car. Ever since moving to Lagniappe, dodging women had become more of a challenge for him than his stint in the Guard—dodging fire in Operation Desert Storm. Give him an earth-to-missile launcher over an interested female any day of the week. And twice on Sundays.

The wind had picked up since he'd arrived at the office around seven. Hot air moving around, just his luck. While all his old buddies were gearing up for snow skiing and racing on snowmobiles in a few months, he'd be stuck in the bayou where the only things sliding about were the snakes and alligators.

As he drove around Lagniappe, Jon debated where to eat. No specialty cafés existed in the little community. The offerings ranged from deep-fried everything to smothered-in-gravy anything. Not that it wasn't good—it was, but he'd love a Runza about now. He could almost taste the homemade dough, stuffed full of flavor, then baked fresh every day. His mouth watered at the thought. Wishful thinking on his part. Sighing, he pulled in front of Cajun's Wharf. At least he could get some boiled shrimp.

He requested a corner table in the back of the room. While he ate, he'd be able to read the entire file on the new case assigned to him and make his notes, and that'd be one less to deal with back at the office.

After being served his iced tea, sans the cup of sugar normally mixed in the glass—what was it with these Southern people and tea so sweet it made his teeth hurt?—he ordered the boiled shrimp, without the "special" house seasonings.

"Would you like a bowl of cayenne on the side, sir?" The waiter scowled at him, disapproval lurking in his young face.

What would he do with a bowl of cayenne? "Um, no thank you."

The waiter gave a curt nod and disappeared, clearly delighted to make his getaway from the strange Yankee. Jon could hear it now, the waiter busting into the kitchen. "Y'all aren't gonna believe the dude sitting at my table. He even ordered unsweetened tea."

Jon opened the file and read the parolee profile.

Caleb Frost: seventeen; incarcerated for sixty days in the Ter-rebonne Parish Juvenile Detention Center in Houma, Louisiana, for illegal Internet downloading; six months probation; scheduled for release—Jon checked the date—today. Great, already a day late and a dollar short. Caleb had been assigned to the Vermilion Parish Parole Office due to receiving new legal guardianship.

Stop the presses! A *new* legal guardian?

That raised red flags in Jon's mind. Minors this close to legal age normally didn't get new guardians. He flipped through the case notes and read on.

Ah, the boy's father died while Caleb was in juvie, an accident on an offshore oil rig. His mother died some years back, leaving him without a parent for a legal guardian. Made sense. So who was the new guardian? A foster family? Those never worked out and Jon often wondered why the courts were so gung ho on shipping these almost-adults around. Just added to the post-trau-matic stress syndrome they all normally suffered from after juvie.

He flipped through more pages until he found the recent court documents. New legal guardian of Caleb Frost was one Sadie Thompson, half sister of the minor.

Jon turned the document over to find the details on Ms. Thompson.

A single woman, longtime resident of Lagniappe, employed by Vermilion Oil, four years into buying her home and twenty-four years of age.

The court had assigned a seventeen-year-old boy to a twenty-four-year-old guardian? A single woman, with no family listed to help her out? Were they serious? Glancing through the paperwork, he realized they were.

The waiter appeared with Jon's lunch. He plopped it onto the table, scowled again, as if Jon had personally insulted him by not ordering the side of cayenne, and scuttled away. Jon took a sip of tea, then went back to the case notes as he ate.

What was such a young, single woman going to do with her brother? Maybe they were close before his incarceration? Jon flipped pages and read the history.

Caleb Frost had lived with his biological father since his parents' divorce eleven years ago. His father had never remarried and according to the notes, there wasn't a woman's influence around Caleb since.

Jon did the math. Caleb had been caught in a man's world since he was six years old. No wonder he'd ended up in juvie. Jon's heart ached for the little boy Caleb had once been.

He peeled and shoved another shrimp into his mouth. Even without the cayenne, seasonings exploded in his mouth. Not just spicy, but a rich blend of seasonings that put his taste buds on notice. He drained his tea and went back to reading.

The boy's attitude hadn't improved in the detention center, apparently. The faculty social worker had ordered a psychological evaluation as well as counseling for him after they'd told him that his father had died. Those notes weren't included in the file. The rest of the report concluded the kid had a high GPA with an aptitude toward computers.

The waiter appeared at Jon's elbow, holding a pitcher. "More tea, sir?"

"Yes, please."

The waiter poured and then withdrew. Jon took another shrimp and continued to read about Caleb Frost's life.

As far as Jon could tell, Caleb had never been around his sister on any basis since the age of six. Yet she was willing to accept guardianship? Jon wondered what kind of young woman would agree to such a thing. Why? It made no sense.

Had she been coerced? Bullied by the court representatives? In his experience, people weren't so willing to step up and accept responsibility for someone they weren't close to unless they had something to gain.

Jon finished his lunch and closed the folder. Well, if he was to be released today, Caleb Frost and his guardian would be coming into his office to set up the parole boundaries.

He intended to monitor this particular relationship carefully.

Very carefully.

TWO

Silence really could be deafening.

Sadie disregarded her brooding brother propped against the wall and concentrated on finding the listing for Jon Garrison's office in the building directory. Why the parole office couldn't be in the state building where she was familiar with everything remained a mystery to her. Why the courthouse?

Because parole officers dealt with criminals.

Shivers attacked her spine as she located the room number and led Caleb to the elevator. The entire ride back to Lagniappe had been conversation-free, and not the comfortable kind, either. Not that she hadn't tried. She'd done her best at sharing, telling her brother about her crisis at work, but no matter what questions she asked, topics she introduced, Caleb hadn't engaged in simple conversation. They'd stopped for lunch at a diner along the way—even there he didn't bother to speak except to grunt out his order for a double cheeseburger and fries. She couldn't put up with this for long.

Off the elevator and down the hall, Caleb remained silent. She came to the door with the number she searched for and pushed it open.

A redheaded lady greeted them. "Can I help y'all?"

Still, Caleb said not a word.

Sadie couldn't put up with this for nine months. She wouldn't. Not with everything going on at work. A sense of being overwhelmed washed over her, yet she smiled at the woman who couldn't be more than her age. "I'm Sadie Thompson and this is my brother, Caleb Frost. He's supposed to report to Mr. Jon Garrison this afternoon."

The woman smiled wide at Caleb. "Hi, Caleb. I'm Lisa, Jon's assistant."

No reaction from Caleb, not even eye contact.

Lisa flashed Sadie a look full of sympathy and winked. "Have a seat. I'll let Jon know you're waiting."

Sadie sat and looked at Caleb, who stood staring out the window. "You could at least try to be polite, yes?"

Her admonishment didn't seem to faze him. He maintained his silence, not even bothering to so much as glance at her.

Frustration chased apprehension around her heart. Sadie pinched the bridge of her nose. She'd known this guardian thing would be difficult, but had no idea just how difficult.

Lord, please give me a clue how to reach him, how to help him.

"Mr. Garrison would like to see you alone first, Ms. Thompson." Lisa stood in the narrow hallway.

Feeling like a child reporting to the principal's office, Sadie stood and followed Lisa to a door off the hall.

"Don't worry, I'll keep an eye on Caleb for you." Lisa shut the door behind her, leaving Sadie to face the principal alone.

Her focus adhered to the man standing behind a desk loaded with manila folders, his hand extended. "Hello, I'm Jon Garrison."

She licked her lips, trying not to stare.

But it was difficult.

He had the wide shoulders of an LSU middle linebacker. His brown hair should've appeared plain, but with the few streaks of gray at his temples, it was anything but. His eyes were that mysterious shade of hazel—not quite green, not quite brown. The only color that came to mind was golden. Yeah, his eyes were warm golden.

"Please, have a seat." He motioned to the chair sitting kitty-corner to his desk and returned to his seat.

She plopped into the hardwood chair that had seen one too

many years in a parish courthouse. Good idea to sit, because all of a sudden, her knees were feeling a little on the mushy side as her old familiar feelings urging her to act on physical attraction began to bubble up.

God, please give me strength.

Jon grabbed a folder, flipped through pages and then shut it. "I have all the information on Caleb and his background." He lifted a pen and tapped it against his chin. "But I have very little on you, aside from the basics."

She stiffened her back. Was she under a microscope now? "Um, what would you like to know?"

"Why did you agree to be Caleb's legal guardian?"

She opened her mouth, hesitated when no words popped out and snapped it shut. What kind of question was that?

The one she'd been asking herself over and over since she'd agreed to this harebrained idea. "Because he's my brother and had nowhere else to go."

"I see." He wrote something on a notebook hiding behind the piles on his desk. "How well do you know your brother, Ms. Thompson?"

Her defenses rose. "I haven't seen Caleb in years, if that's what you're asking." What was this, the Spanish Inquisition? She'd been approached by the court, not the other way around. "He's my half brother."

"Yes, I'm aware." He smiled, the power of it nearly knocking her over. "Were you two close before his incarceration in the juvenile center?"

"Not really. He lived with his father."

"But were you close?"

Boy, he sure pushed every button available. "I saw Caleb once since he moved in with his father. At our mother's funeral seven years ago."

He laid his pen on the desk. "I'm sorry. I didn't mean to offend."

"No offense taken." Yet. *God, please. I'm following You the best I know how. Help me out with this guy. Please.*

"I'm just trying to determine what's best for Caleb. Naturally, I need to know your motivation for accepting custody."

"What's best for Caleb is that he doesn't become a ward of the state, which he would have had I not agreed to be his guardian."

"I see." And his tone clearly implied he did.

She tried again. "I'm giving him a second chance, Mr. Garrison. He made a mistake and he's paying for it. He deserves the opportunity to put his life back on track, yes?" And didn't she know that was a hard road to walk.

Mr. Garrison remained silent, just staring at her.

She ducked her head to avoid the judgment in his stare. Bad girl Sadie takes in her criminal brother—which one is the worse influence on the other? "I spent six months in a foster home after my mother died before I turned eighteen. I know how horrible that feels. I don't want Caleb to have to go through that."

"Ms. Thompson, I'm not here to make your life difficult. My job is to help Caleb in adjusting back into society. I need to know all the facts surrounding every aspect of his life to help him be successful. That includes knowing about the adult responsible for him and their relationship."

She rigidly held her tears in check and met his gaze. "I understand. I just want you to know I'm trying to help him, too. Give him every opportunity to set himself straight." No one had believed Uncle Joe had turned his life around after his incarceration and look what'd happened—he'd committed suicide.

"Then we have the same goal." He glanced down at his notebook. "The juvenile center sent you home with a schedule, correct?"

"Of times he has to visit you and the therapist, yes. We'll be registering him for the summer school session as soon as we leave here."

"Very good. I'll come by later this week for a home visit."

Her heart leaped into her throat. "A home visit? This week?"

He cocked his head. "Is that a problem?"

"No. It just wasn't on the schedule."

"Home visits are unscheduled, Ms. Thompson. It allows us to view the parolee in their environment. Gauge how they're adjusting and building relationships."

Building relationships? Not even a full day with Caleb and already she'd failed in that aspect. "O-Okay."

He flashed a smile that warmed her to her toes as he stood. "Great. I think I'll talk to Caleb now. If you wouldn't mind sending him in on your way out?"

Dismissed. Nothing new for her.

She struggled to get her feet under her. "It was nice meeting you." Even though being in his presence had been unsettling.

"We'll be seeing each other quite often."

What did he mean by that? Did he think she'd require more monitoring than usual? She barely knew the man and already he'd judged her to be an incompetent guardian. Based upon what?

God, I don't understand.

Sadie entered the waiting room, and Lisa jumped to her feet from her seat beside Caleb. "Come on, Caleb. I'll take you to meet Jon. He's a nice guy. I think you'll like him. Most of the teens do."

Her brother shoved to his feet, silently following the rambling young woman. Sadie pulled her cell phone free from its clip and glanced at the screen. Two missed calls. Probably from Georgia.

Deacon was right to be concerned. As the only locally owned and operated oil company operating in the parish, Vermilion Oil employed several hundred workers. Between fifty and seventy oil wells produced into each of the sabotaged facilities, but when the facility went down, all wells producing into it stopped production. Halted production meant layoffs. Additionally, the company had recently put in new, state-of-the-art monitoring systems that enabled them to operate the facilities with less manpower. They were already dealing with protests from workers laid off after that decision. More layoffs would just add fuel to the fire. All in all, it was a mess.

She pressed the number to check her voice mail. She'd been right—both calls came from Georgia. The manner of sabotage on this latest facility matched the other one—tank valve tampering. Not a single witness because both facilities had automatic controls rather than employees on-site. The automatic controls shut down the facility in the event of a malfunction. Yet the chances of two facilities having the tank valves tampered with wasn't a coincidence. No, this was deliberate.

Knowing how to get around the new systems, how to tamper with the valves just enough to damage the facility but not cause any environmental damage...had to be an inside job. But who and why?

Deacon hadn't been able to get the first facility repaired yet as the coordinating law enforcement agencies were still investigating. Which left Vermilion Oil in a very bad position.

And Sadie, as head of public relations for the company, in a very precarious spot.

She took a seat and called her contact at the paper to reserve space for a statement, left a message on voice mail and then pulled out a pad and pen from her purse. She'd barely make the five o'clock cutoff, even if she hurried. With rapid speed she wrote out a press release, assuring the good citizens of Lagniappe that Mr. Wynn intended to beef up security on all of Vermilion Oil's wells and facilities, as well as launch a full investigation on his own because the law enforcement agencies had yet to uncover a suspect. Now to convince Deacon he had to do just that.

Finished, she chewed the end of her pen and reread her words. Her statement would appease some of the general public, but not all. She made a note to ask Deacon for a complete list of all the workers at both facilities and the maintenance employees on each of the wells. Hopefully, there'd be a single name attached to all. If not, the news wasn't good.

That would mean a conspiracy against Vermilion Oil.

Jon jotted notes in his file as he waited for Caleb. He hadn't quite formed an opinion of the new guardian yet. At least, not that he could file in his report.

Sadie was quite a looker. Her tawny hair hung down midback,

looking soft and silky. Yet it'd been the pain and distrust lurking in her eyes that had pulled such a response from his gut. Her vulnerability reached into the hidden places of his heart and took hold.

He recognized her look, both from his service in the National Guard and his time logged as a parole officer. It was the look of desperation and despair.

But she was the guardian of one of his charges. He wouldn't allow himself to respond to her emotionally, or he'd lose his objectivity.

The door swung open, ripping him from his thoughts. A young man shuffled in. As tall as Jon himself, the boy wore his hardships on his shoulders like a saggy sweatshirt.

Jon's heart sunk to his feet. He'd seen this type too many times before—this wouldn't be an easy parolee.

"Hi, Caleb. Jon Garrison." He extended his hand.

The boy glanced at it, paused and then gave him a hard stare.

So that's how it was going to be—distrustful and full of attitude. Jon dropped his hand and motioned to the chair. He couldn't really blame him. Juvie didn't exactly instill good social relations. "Have a seat."

Caleb hesitated, as if debating if he'd been given a choice. He finally slumped onto the chair, stretching out his long legs in front of him.

Jon recognized the body language—loner attitude, appearance of disgust, contempt for all adults... Caleb exhibited each and every one. In spades from every fiber of his being. He'd be a difficult one to crack, hard to rehabilitate. Not only for Jon, but also for his guardian.

Jon's heart went out to Sadie. She'd unwittingly been saddled with a serious problem and probably didn't even realize it yet.

"You know the procedure, right? The social worker at the center explained it all to you upon your release, correct?"

Caleb glared at him, his eyes narrowed.

Jon stared back. He had to take control. "Right?"

The boy crossed his arms and stared at the wall behind Jon.

Jon released a slow breath. "Caleb, you don't have to like me or anybody else, but you do have to answer my questions."

"I was told."

At last, the boy spoke. Jon smiled and leaned forward, making himself more approachable. "Do you have any questions? You can ask me anything. I'm here to help you."

"Why do I hafta go to summer school?"

"Because you missed the last five weeks of your junior year. You have to make up what you missed or you won't be considered a senior come the fall semester."

Caleb grunted.

Jon tried again to shove open the door of communication. "Any other questions?"

"How long do I gotta live with her?"

Two questions. Progress. "You mean with your sister?"

"She ain't my sister."

"She's not?" Jon lifted a file and pretended to search for a certain piece of paper. "I'm sure that's what the court report said."

"She's my half sister."

"Oh." Jon put the folder back on the desk and tented his hands. "Well, she's still your legal guardian."

"Not by choice." Belligerence covered the boy's words and presence. Another common thread in those from juvie—the dislike of not having control and resenting those who had it.

Jon cleared his throat. "Not yours, no, but hers. She agreed to take you on, Caleb. I'd say that was pretty generous of her."

Caleb dropped his gaze back to the floor. Anger or fear? Both were strong emotions and could trigger bad behavior. Violent, even.

"I see." This time, Jon did look at his notes. "Well, you're on probation for six months."

"I'll be eighteen before then."

"Yes, you will. At such time, your sister will be removed as your legal guardian and you'll be responsible for adhering to the guidelines for your supervision yourself." Unless he was already back in detention. Judging by Caleb's attitude, Jon had his doubts the boy would straighten up.

"Yeah, I was told that, too."

"Good." Jon stood and let out a sigh. "As I told your sister, expect a home visit this week."

Caleb rose and slouched, not answering.

One more try… "You know, this whole process goes much easier if you work with us instead of against us."

"You don't know me. Don't know anything about me." Caleb grabbed for the door. "Are we done?"

Jon shook his head. Ungrateful, selfish… Kids like this were all too common. They thought about no one but themselves. "Yes, we're done. I'll see you this week at home."

The teen left without a word.

Many years and cases ago, Jon had given up the idea that all parolees could be rehabilitated. Despite counseling and social workers, juvies were the worst. Once they'd started down the wrong path in life, it seemed they couldn't recover. His job was to ensure they didn't break any other laws on his watch. The odds of their turning over a new leaf were nearly impossible.

Jon knew all too well how rare rehabilitation truly was. He'd been *raised* by an aunt who couldn't be interrupted from her partying—drinking and spending time with numerous men—to see to it that he had anything to eat. Maybe Aunt Torey was the reason he'd gone into career paths to help others. But what he'd seen of the system hadn't changed his opinion. People didn't change all that often.

He opened Caleb's file again. Music and movie pirating, hmm? Not so serious a crime, but becoming more and more common with teens. No telling what he'd been exposed to inside the detention center. Most of those places, like prison, taught people how to be criminals. Well, Jon would order the full record from the center and see what Caleb had been up to while detained. Maybe he'd been in trouble before and managed not to get caught. But it'd only be a matter of time before Jon uncovered the truth and learned if there was any hope of Caleb Frost's reentry to society as a viable member.

THREE

"Ms. Thompson, what is Vermilion Oil doing to discover who's behind the sabotaging of your facilities and rigs? This is the second incident. Surely the company is deeply concerned. Damaged equipment could lead to leaks into the bayou, killing uncountable wildlife."

Sadie glanced across the slew of media personnel to meet the imposing stare of Jackson Devereaux, investigative reporter from The New Orleans *Times-Picayune* and husband of Lagniappe's own Alyssa LeBlanc-Devereaux. Sweat pooled under Sadie's blouse. If the New Orleans paper had sent their hotshot reporter, then Deacon's fears of a media frenzy were realized and the company *was* in more trouble than she'd imagined.

Yesterday had been stressful enough just getting Caleb to his appointments and home. On top of that, Deacon hadn't been satisfied with her press release. So dissatisfied, he'd scheduled a press conference for first thing this muggy Tuesday morning. Time to sink or swim.

She cleared her throat and met Jackson's stare head-on. "Of course we're very concerned over these blatant acts of sabotage. It's an outrage. Vermilion Oil is working with the sheriff's office, the Department of Environmental Quality, the state Department of Natural Resources and the state police in their investigations into these damages. We will not tolerate such destruction."

"But what is the company doing on its own?" Jackson

elbowed past another reporter, inching closer to the podium. "Surely y'all are conducting an independent investigation? These are, after all, *your* facilities being damaged. And it's happened twice."

Heat crept up Sadie's neck, but she refused to buckle under such scrutiny. She jutted out her chin and resisted the urge to blow her bangs off her forehead. "I can assure you, Mr. Devereaux, Vermilion Oil is undertaking a full internal investigation. I'm not at liberty to discuss the details of our endeavors at this time. But be certain of this, we won't stop investigating until the culprits have been discovered and justice has been served."

"Ms. Thompson, does law enforcement have any suspects?" A local reporter jostled to push next to Mr. Devereaux. Vying for a spot and attention, even though she could very well take the information straight off the printed press release handed out moments ago.

"I'm not at liberty to discuss suspects, Ms. Martin. I'd suggest you talk to Sheriff Theriot in regards to the sheriff's department's investigation."

And let him take some of the heat.

"Are any other companies being targeted by these saboteurs? Could this be an act of terrorism?"

Sadie's mouth went dry as she locked stares with the reporter from Shreveport, Louisiana. "That'd be another question for law enforcement. I'm only involved with the investigation regarding the damaged facilities belonging to Vermilion Oil."

"What does this mean for Mr. Wynn?"

Sadie sought the reporter who'd asked the question. Her gaze fell on the young man from Alexandria. "Mr. Bosworth." She gave a nod to the business and finance reporter. Oh, this could be very bad for Deacon. "Mr. Wynn is forging ahead with business as usual. Currently, Vermilion Oil has eight facilities working properly in this parish alone. Security on every site has been heightened, and, of course, we have our thorough background check system for every employee working on the rigs themselves and in the facilities. This won't happen again." It couldn't.

The reporter all but rolled his eyes, but Sadie didn't have time to elaborate before the next reporter shouted out a question. "Ms. Thompson, we've heard some say the layoffs of several workers has led to improper monitoring, contributing to these incidents. Would you care to comment?"

Vultures—like buzzards after a wounded animal. "I can attest that every possible measure is being taken to ensure this doesn't happen again."

"It's said that Vermilion Oil's presence in the bayou is causing havoc in the local fishermen and hunters' businesses." The young hotshot from Lake Charles thrust his recorder closer to the podium. "There's a local group who's demanding Vermilion Oil close down the wells in the bayou to protect the environment. Would you care to comment?"

Sadie held up her hands. "I'm sorry, that's all I have for the moment. Thank you so much for your time." She gave a curt nod. "Good day."

The reporters continued to throw questions at her back as she made her way inside the main office. Behind the tinted windows, Deacon Wynn paced the polished floors. "They're pouncing on us, Sadie. Profits are down. I'm losing money hand over fist right now. Over two hundred of my oil rigs have no facility to produce into. Every day they're down, I'm losing hundreds of thousands of dollars."

She let out a sigh and gripped her leather appointment book tighter. "It'll bounce back up, Deacon." *Lord, please let it be so.*

"You sure about that? The damage to the facilities is costly. That's cutting into our operating costs." He ran his fingers through his thinning hair. "We can't afford for another to go down. Especially not to sabotage. They've knocked out almost a quarter of our top-producing rigs. I can't afford to stay in business at this rate."

Sadie's heart twisted. Deacon Wynn was a hard and cunning

businessman, but he was also a good man. He was one of the few men who'd never made a pass at her, despite her reputation. He appreciated her talent in public relations, giving her chances that no other business owner in Lagniappe would have ever provided her. She owed him. Big-time. She'd have to make him take her suggestions this time—to save his company. "We need to bring in some independent investigator to look into the sabotage, sir. Someone who'll take this situation very seriously and hopefully can make progress where law enforcement seems to be stumped."

Deacon stared out the window at the departing press. "You think an independent could do anything more than what law enforcement is doing?" Deacon shook his head. "We need a miracle. I need answers. And fast. If we leak anything into the waterways, it'll cost me millions for cleanup, which will put the company in bankruptcy."

"We have to do *something*, Deacon." She glanced at the cars leaving the parking lot. "We know some of the laid-off workers have an ax to grind with us. I'll start working on that angle."

He nodded, but didn't take his gaze from the windows. "Whatever it takes. We can't afford for anything else to go wrong."

"Dad."

Both Sadie and Deacon turned as Lance Wynn strode toward them. His hair had been trimmed since the last time Sadie had seen the young man. He wore jeans that hung low on his hips and a T-shirt that needed a better washing. But his face appeared clear. Maybe rehab had done him some good.

He reached his father. "I'm sorry to hear about this latest incident. What can I do to help?"

Deacon's brows formed a firm line. "I'm surprised to see you here. Thought you were no longer interested in the company or me."

Lance's Adam's apple bobbed. "Personal differences aside, you're my father and this is your company. When someone lashes out at you, I take it personally."

"Like you have with Candy-Jo?" Deacon shook his head.

"Never mind. Like I told you last week, I don't want you here, Lance. We've said all there is to say between us."

"But, Dad, I can help. I've hung around these outfits since I was ten years old. I know the business from the ground up. Let me try to help." Desperation hung in the kid's tone.

Deacon's brows formed a firm line. "I thought I made it perfectly clear that you weren't welcome on any Vermilion Oil property. Do you want me to call security?"

Sadie took a step backward. Ever since Deacon had married Candy-Jo two years ago, there'd been conflict in the family. Candy-Jo was a much younger woman, and Sadie had heard the tension in the family had gotten so bad that eighteen-year-old Lance had gotten into some sort of mess with drugs and checked into a rehab center. Not that Deacon had ever discussed it with her. He didn't talk much about his personal business.

Deacon addressed her directly, ignoring his son. "Keep me updated, Sadie. I'm counting on you to get this handled." He spun and strode to the elevators, but Sadie detected a slight sluggishness to his step.

Lance stood still, silently staring at his father's retreating back.

She ran her finger along a rough seam on her leather notebook. Deacon's health had taken a nosedive over the last several months. No wonder—his new wife and his son didn't get along, and the family sat in utter turmoil. Rumor had it that Deacon had even written Lance out of his will. And now these sabotages plagued Deacon's business. Poor man, how much more could he take?

"Let me help you. I know the people and the business," Lance said.

She chewed the inside corner of her mouth. Lance *had* learned the business from the ground up and might have connections with the field workers. But, as desperate as she was right now, Sadie couldn't involve him without Deacon's permission. She let out a soft sigh. "I appreciate the offer, but I don't think so."

Lance hung his head.

Her cell phone saved her from any further conversation with the young man. She flipped the phone open. "Hello?"

"This is Ms. Mitchell from Lagniappe High with the summer school program. Is this Caleb Frost's guardian?"

Sadie's heart thumped quicker. "Yes, I'm Caleb Frost's guardian. How can I help you?" She smiled at Lance before turning and heading back to her office.

Interesting.

Jon turned off the television as soon as the press conference faded to the news anchor's commentary and tossed the remote onto the desk. Sadie Thompson had grit, he had to give her that. There was something about her, something that seemed to resonate deep inside him. Knowing she'd just undertaken an enormous burden with Caleb, Jon had to admire her spunk shown at the press conference for Vermilion Oil. It was time he found out more about Sadie Thompson.

But Vermilion Oil... Something about the company—where had he seen it mentioned recently? Not the newscasts of the troubles the company had. Something else nagged him. He just couldn't figure out from where.

"Hey, boss, here are the sheets for today's appointments." Lisa handed him a folder as she cocked out her hip, disrupting any chance of concentration that he'd mustered. "Another busy day. You have field visits this morning, then four appointments after lunch."

"Thanks." He nodded toward the TV. "Have you heard about those sabotages over at Vermilion Oil?"

She shook her head. "No, but a side reference to Vermilion Oil's in there." She dropped the local daily on his desk. "Did you see today's top story?"

Other than the oil company's issues, what could the hot news be—a church bake sale? He bit back his sarcasm. He glanced at the captions. "What?"

"A murder. Some man killed just outside Lagniappe early this morning. Shot deader than a doorknob."

In today's world, the news wasn't shocking. But in a small community, murders didn't happen all the time. He scanned the article. The man, Harold Daniels, worked as a facility manager for Vermilion Oil. Found dead out off Harden Lane in the early hours of the morning, shot in the chest. Local sheriff had no comment.

Jon shook his head. "It's sad what the world's coming to."

"Makes you realize how short and precious life can be. Makes you want to live every moment to the fullest, yes?" Lisa gave a sad smile.

"I suppose so." For a moment, Sadie's image floated across his mind.

"Jon." Lisa's voice held uncertainty.

He glanced up. "Yes?"

"I don't like to gossip or anything, but about Caleb Frost's new guardian?"

Sadie. "Yes?"

"Well…do you know her history?"

"Just what was in the file."

"I see." Her face scrunched into a scowl.

"What is it, Lisa?"

"I don't know her personally or anything, but she has somewhat of a reputation around town."

Something lodged sideways in Jon's throat. He swallowed hard. "What kind of reputation?"

"Just that she used to be a heavy drinker. And, uh, let's say she, uh, *dated* quite a few of the men in town."

His gut clenched. Sadie was like Aunt Torey?

"I heard she changed and all, but I just thought you might want to know." Lisa shrugged. "It might be important to Caleb's rehabilitation."

He handed Lisa back the newspaper and reached for his briefcase. "Thanks. Guess I'd better get to today's field visits."

"Sure. I'll hold the fort."

He glanced at the itinerary she'd given him. Sadie Thompson and Caleb Frost weren't on the list for a home visit. Probably a good thing. He hadn't been able to get her out of his mind. Now, after hearing Lisa's report, he had to wonder why.

No, he wouldn't even start trying to analyze why he kept thinking about Sadie Thompson. He had a job to do and as he crossed the lobby to the parking lot, he was determined to do just that—his job and nothing more.

Two hours and four visits later, Jon pulled into the café for a quick salad. A blast of frigid air hit his face as he opened the door. Ah, the pricelessness of air-conditioning on a sweltering July day.

He nodded to a couple of the townspeople as he made his way to the swivel stools against the bar counter. No one greeted him or even tossed him a welcoming smile. He'd lived in Lagniappe over a year—when would the locals warm up to him?

After placing his order, Jon sipped his water and studied the people around him. Most were on their lunch breaks, as well, wearing the fashions of their jobs. Uniforms for the minimum-wagers, dirty jeans and T-shirts for the manual laborers and suits for the numerous professionals hanging out their shingles in the small town. Jon felt out of place in his khaki slacks and polo-style shirt.

"Man, Deacon Wynn's gonna be outta business soon," one of the men in a dirt-streaked shirt mumbled to his lunch partner.

"Would serve him right. That family's got delusions they're above all the rest of us." The other worker splashed ketchup over his mountain of fries.

"Yeah, but didn't stop his son from getting into trouble, did it?"

"Heard he'd gotten into drugs and gone into rehab. Shows that money can buy trouble, that's for sure."

Jon tightened his grip on his water glass. That's where he recognized the name *Vermilion Oil*. One of his probationers was the son of Deacon Wynn. Rehab? No, the boy had been in juvie, turning eighteen less than a week after his release.

Lance Wynn was a good kid, basically. Raised in a family with too much money and not enough attention. He'd dabbled in drugs, gotten caught and sent to juvie. He only had another month of probation, then that record would be closed and sealed. A past swept under the carpet, unlike the less wealthy juvies.

It never ceased to amaze Jon what having money could do.

Today had been the day to beat all days.

Sadie grabbed her purse from the passenger seat and headed to the front porch. That draining press conference had set the tone for her entire day, followed by Caleb missing the bus and having to walk to school, arriving for class late, which explained the call from the principal this morning. The only thing good about today was no new facility had been damaged. She yearned for a hot bath and an early bedtime.

Unfortunately, she had to cook something for supper so Caleb could eat. Not that he'd appreciate her efforts—he hadn't since he'd come home.

Home. As if Caleb would ever consider her house home. In spite of her numerous attempts the previous day, he'd made it perfectly clear he had no desire to seek out any type of relationship with her. Period. Stony silence and simple yes-and-no answers were the extent of their rapport.

Sadie sighed and grabbed the mail before reaching for the front door. Caleb couldn't be bothered to bring in the mail. She turned the knob. Or lock the door, apparently. She nearly tripped over his size-twelve sneakers lying just inside the foyer.

"Caleb!"

"Yo." The grunt came from the living room.

As if she didn't know where to find him. The television blared screeching guitars from some music station. For the millionth time in barely forty-eight hours, she considered canceling her satellite service. The constant rock video after rock video would drive her insane.

"You need to keep your shoes out from in front of the door."

"Whatever."

She clenched her jaw and headed to the kitchen. No matter what she did, nothing reached him. Caleb just didn't care.

Tossing her purse onto the buffet, she sifted through the mail. Sale papers and envelopes addressed to resident found their way into the trash. Oh, yippee, an insurance premium notice—how lucky could she be?

She stopped at the last envelope. Plain white, no return address. Closer inspection revealed no stamp or postmark, either. Just her name and address in bold, block letters in black on the front. Odd.

Sadie slit open the back and withdrew the contents.

A Polaroid fell facedown on the counter. She turned over the picture and gasped. A man with lifeless eyes stared into the camera. What in the world? She dropped the photograph and reached for the newspaper clipping.

Not just a clipping—an obituary with today's date. A Harold Daniels. She stared at the man's grainy picture in the paper. She didn't recognize him.

Wait a minute, she knew that name...he worked for her company, but she'd never met him before. Why would someone send her an obituary of someone she didn't know?

She grabbed the Polaroid and compared the photographs.

Same man!

Icy fingers trailed her back.

She set the clipping on the counter and unfolded the piece of paper. Her hands trembled so badly, she almost couldn't read the letter.

Same bold, black, block letters as on the envelope. Sadie pressed her lips together, holding her breath as she read.

YOUR BROTHER WILL BE NEXT IF YOU DON'T DO EXACTLY AS YOU ARE TOLD. INSTRUCTIONS TO FOLLOW SOON. DO NOT NOTIFY THE POLICE. WAIT TO HEAR FROM US.

The paper drifted from her slack fingers.
Dear Lord, help me.

FOUR

The sun crested to midsky, shining down on the little town of Lagniappe. Midweek. Not that Sadie took the time to notice.

The letter, obituary and photograph invaded her mind this Wednesday morning, just as it had tormented her all night.

Sadie sat at her desk on the third floor. Drilling production reports littered her in-box, but she couldn't concentrate. Couldn't even think.

Georgia dropped a folder onto the desk. "That's the info on the laid-off workers you wanted. I couldn't see anything important in there."

"Merci." She opened the file and scrolled through the names. Most were men she'd known for years, some intimately. Reaching for her pen, she crossed off the names of those who'd already found alternate work. When she'd finished, she marked off those who had officially retired. That left a total of twenty-nine names. She shoved the list into her purse.

But Sadie couldn't concentrate on the next step in the investigation. Her mind couldn't focus on Vermilion Oil and its problems. Instead, her mind filled with words from the letter.

What could they want? She didn't have any money, that much was for sure. Especially since taking in Caleb.

And what about the timing? Caleb had been with her for only two days and now a blackmail letter? It didn't make sense.

She'd hidden the envelope with the revolting contents in her purse last night, then went about her evening as if the evil wasn't there. Caleb hadn't bothered to thank her for the stir-fry she'd thrown together nor had he offered to help load the dishwasher.

Sleep had eluded her. She'd opened the envelope and read the letter again and again. Sadie could recite it from memory.

YOUR BROTHER WILL BE NEXT IF YOU DON'T DO EXACTLY AS YOU ARE TOLD.

Who knew Caleb lived with her? She didn't have any friends outside of her church. Even her coworkers didn't get too close, except Georgia. Trying to live down a bad reputation was like trying to cover up the stench of the bayou—not easily accomplished. She'd shared only with Pastor Spencer Bertrand her decision to step up as Caleb's guardian, but he wouldn't have said anything to anyone.

Would he?

INSTRUCTIONS TO FOLLOW SOON.

What kind of instructions? Frustration sat in her temples. She rubbed her forehead, attempting to ward off the approaching migraine to no avail.

Instructions for what? What did they want from her? She had nothing. She barely made her mortgage and utilities every month. Maybe she'd been stupid in trying to buy a house, but she was sick of throwing away money in rent every month. She'd cleaned out her savings for the down payment.

"I need to see Mr. Wynn. The receptionist said his office was up here on the third floor. Can you direct me to him?"

Sadie jerked her attention to the sheriff standing in her office doorway. She'd been so lost in thought, she hadn't even noticed him standing there.

DON'T NOTIFY THE POLICE.

She pasted on a smile. "May I ask what about?"

"One of his employees was murdered last night. I need to ask him a few questions."

Her stomach cramped, just knowing the blackmail letter was in her purse. "Certainly." She nodded. "Take a left down the hall and he's the second office on the right. His secretary shouldn't have left for lunch yet."

"Merci."

Sabotage and now murdered employees...what could be next? Watching the sheriff leave, a sense of loneliness washed over Sadie that she hadn't felt in several months. No one to turn to. No one to share with. No one to ease the burdens of life. The emotions clogged her throat.

WAIT TO HEAR FROM US.

Hear from them how? When?

Brring! Brring!

Sadie jumped and stared at the phone sitting on the desk. Would they call her?

The light blinked, indicating someone had answered the line. She let out the long breath she hadn't realized she'd been holding.

Scared of a ringing phone? Enough was enough!

Sadie snatched her purse, slung the strap over her shoulder and headed out the door. No one stopped her to ask where she was going. It didn't matter, she could take lunch whenever she felt like it.

Summer had blazed into Lagniappe with the wilting of the tulips. Temperatures hovered in the upper nineties. Flowers burst forth through the greenery. All seemed a promise of better things to come.

Except just when she'd made strides in her new life, here she was, being blackmailed.

She drove the short distance to the café. Not that she was

hungry, but she needed to eat. She'd managed to shove down only some of the vegetables from the stir-fry last night.

The hostess sat her at a table next to a window. She ordered the shrimp salad and iced tea from the waitress, then stared out the window.

DO NOT NOTIFY THE POLICE.

As if. She'd spent too many years avoiding them and old habits died hard. But she needed to tell someone. Who? Pastor? No, she wouldn't drag him into this. He'd be obligated, at least morally if not legally, to tell the police. Georgia? No, she couldn't drag her only friend into this mess. The loneliness threatened to suffocate Sadie.

"Ms. Thompson."

Sadie jumped, nearly spilling tea in her lap. She glanced up to see Jon Garrison silhouetted by the midday sun streaking through the window. Her heart pounded. "Mr. Garrison."

"How are you today?"

"F-Fine." Why was she stuttering like an imbecile?

"How's Caleb?"

"Good. In summer school." Oh, great, she blabbered, too. Nerves bunched in her stomach. She needed to calm down, get a grip. He couldn't know about the letter.

But what if he found out? Would they take Caleb away, make him a ward of the state? She couldn't let that happen. She wouldn't.

"That's good." He paused as the waitress delivered Sadie's salad and retreated. "Well, I'll leave you in peace. Enjoy your lunch."

Words wouldn't form. She nodded and let him walk away.

She couldn't tell anyone about the letter. If anyone found out, especially the police, her brother would end up back in the system. Her experience with foster homes didn't exactly fill her with warm and fuzzy memories. Rather, she recalled the physical and sexual abuse. No, despite her and Caleb's awkward relationship, she'd never let that happen to him.

Never.

She'd handle this on her own, just like she always had. One way or another, she'd figure out what to do. She had to tell Caleb. Maybe he could help her think of who could send her such a letter.

Whoever sent the letter was a murderer, that much was certain.

And now he was in Sadie's life.

Going back to work was as useless as trying to figure out alone who the blackmailer was and what he wanted.

Sadie called her office and told Deacon she'd developed an upset stomach at lunch. Wasn't that the truth? Just having the envelope in her purse made her sick. And running into Jon Garrison... She didn't need the distraction of the man right now.

After rushing home, she stood under the hot water spray, letting the steam unclog the cobwebs of her mind. Maybe she'd never hear from the blackmailer again. But then, she'd live her life in fear, wondering when it would come.

The phone rang, nearly scaring her out of her skin. She grabbed her cell from her purse and tightened the belt of her robe. "Hello?"

"Hey, there. Are you feeling better?" Georgia asked.

"A little." She grabbed the paper half in/half out of her purse.

"Good. I set up your meeting with the local whiners for tomorrow afternoon. Their *spokesman* showed up on our doorstep this afternoon, demanding the wells be removed from the bayou before we polluted the local wildlife."

"Oh, good gravy." The marsh wells and facilities occupied less than thirty acres, a small percentage of fishing and hunting area. These local loons were making a stink over nothing, at a time when Vermilion Oil didn't need any more bad publicity. "What time?"

"Three. I've already requested reports on fishing and hunting, as well as wildlife population numbers on the bayou areas we have wells in."

"You're a lifesaver, Georgia. Thanks." She fingered the edge of the list of names she'd taken from the office.

"No problemo. You get to feeling better so I don't have to fill in for you tomorrow. Later, girl."

Sadie laughed and hung up the phone, then immediately picked it back up and dialed. So much for not being able to work. She had to act now.

Twenty-nine names of workers who'd been laid off because of technology. Twenty-nine men who could be sabotaging the facilities.

And twenty-nine possibilities of blackmailers.

She'd made it through eight calls—all people whom she'd been able to eliminate as suspects—when a door slammed, then the television blared at full volume.

Caleb had come home from school.

Quickly dressing in jeans and a T-shirt, she stuffed the blackmail letter into her pocket and headed down the hall. Even if her brother wasn't responding to her attempts to bond with him, he was involved with what tormented her mind. It was time to seek his input. She couldn't do this alone.

She entered the living room to find Caleb watching yet another music video channel. "How was your day?"

He grunted, his attention focused on the flashing lights on the television.

She withdrew the envelope from her pocket just as the video spewed out a tirade of profanity.

Gritting her teeth, Sadie fought to disguise her annoyance. "Caleb, you know the house rules—nothing with profanity."

"Fine. I'm going to my room. At least there I can listen to what I want." Caleb pressed the remote and moved to stomp down the hall.

"Wait." Her voice echoed loud against the sudden silence. "I need to show you something. Talk to you about it."

Caleb let out a heavy sigh and faced her. "What now?" Belligerence creeped into those two words like a bar's neon sign.

With a trembling hand, she passed him the envelope. "I received this yesterday."

He scanned the letter, the obituary, and stared at the picture. "Who is this?"

"A guy who worked for my company, but I didn't know him personally."

What felt like an eternity later, he lifted his gaze to hers. The indifference he normally wore like a shield had morphed into something else. Hurt? Shock? "Where'd you get this?"

Little pinpricks dotted Sadie's arms. "It was in the mailbox yesterday." She swallowed hard. "But I don't understand. You just got here. No one knew you were coming to live with me."

He tossed the envelope's contents onto the coffee table and ran a hand over his face. "I sure didn't tell anybody and I don't know anyone in this nothing town."

She eased to perch on the arm of the chair. "Then who knew you were here? What do they want?"

He shrugged.

"I'm open to any ideas." Sadie clasped her hands tightly in her lap.

"Sorry, don't have a clue."

"Caleb, we're in this together."

"I don't know what you want me to say."

What could she do? She gave him a shaky smile and rested her hand on his shoulder. He didn't flinch away. "Don't worry about it. I'll handle it."

"Can I go to my room now?"

Tears burning her eyes, she nodded. He ambled down the hall. Moments later, his door slammed shut and earsplitting music once again filled the house.

Sadie hauled in a deep breath and pinched the bridge of her nose. *Dear Lord, I sure could use some help.*

Nothing but the thumping beat of Caleb's music answered her, but she knew she wasn't alone, and that knowledge comforted her. With a sigh, she shoved the letter, picture and clipping back into the envelope. She worried the corner with her thumbnail as she considered her options.

She had no choice but to wait and be contacted again.

A sensation of helplessness washed over her. Waiting. That particular virtue had never been her strong point. Now she had no choice but to wait and see what happened next.

Wandering into the kitchen, she tossed the envelope on the counter and began to prepare supper. Caleb's attitude about the letter gave her some hope—at least he talked *to* her instead of at her. Maybe they could create a normal sibling relationship after all. Hadn't Pastor Bertrand told her to look for the blessings in every situation?

A pounding on the front door rose over the beat of the music.

Her heart quickened. Were the blackmailers here with their demands?

Sadie shook her head, mentally chiding herself. Blackmailers were cowards who wanted something for nothing. They didn't show up at the door and knock politely. She wiped her hands and opened the front door.

Jon Garrison's wide shoulders filled the doorway. He wore a crooked grin, again causing the weak-kneed reaction. "Hello, Ms. Thompson."

Oh, no, she couldn't react to his mere presence in such a way, especially because he had to be here for a home visit. The house was a mess—Caleb's things thrown about as she'd refused to play maid and pick up after him, Sunday's newspaper scattered across the coffee table, the coupons she'd cut lying on the end table. She swallowed. "Hello, Mr. Garrison."

"I think we're beyond the formality. Please, call me Jon."

She couldn't just leave him standing on the porch. Pulling open the door, she waved him inside. "Then call me Sadie."

His gaze darted around the room. What could he be thinking? She glanced into the living room, trying to see it through his eyes. Secondhand furniture. Scuffed and scratched floors. Threadbare rugs. Cheap curtains.

Her back stiffened. Why should she care what he thought? She did the best she could. She didn't owe him any explanations.

The aroma of fried shrimp filled the air.

"Hang on. I was fixing supper when you knocked." Sadie rushed to the kitchen, grabbed the slotted spoon and turned the shrimp in the hot grease.

"Smells good."

She jumped and glanced over her shoulder. Jon had followed her into the kitchen. What would he think of her feeding Caleb shrimp po'boys for supper? Was that considered a good meal for a teen?

Hating that she second-guessed herself and feeling like she was constantly under scrutiny, she opened the fridge and pulled out the makings for a salad.

Jon leaned against the counter, making her nervous with his stare logging her every move. "How is Caleb adjusting to summer school?"

If only she had an answer. "Fine." At least, that's how she chose to interpret her brother's replying grunts to her questions.

"Good. The counselor said he attended all his classes today, so that's a good start."

Her hands froze over the iceberg lettuce. "You talked to his counselor?"

Jon nodded. "Always check up on my charges after their first day or so. It's a good indication if they actually make it to all their classes."

"Hmm." She popped the core from the head and set the lettuce in the colander. "I think Caleb will do just fine. He's a smart kid, yes?" From what she remembered, anyway. And she prayed he would do well.

"How're you two getting along?"

She couldn't lie—as soon as Caleb walked into the room, Jon would know their relationship was strained. "We're in an adjustment period."

Jon laughed. "That's an interesting way to answer the question."

His laughter did the strangest things to her—made her remember the feelings from her past. No, she was changed.

Attraction was one thing, as long as she didn't let it lead her to morally suspect behaviour. And while Jon might make her feel things she'd thought forgotten, he wasn't exactly relationship material. How could he be? He had the power of her brother's immediate future. Not a good basis for a romance. Besides, she didn't even know if he was a Christian!

Spooning the shrimp out and plopping them onto a paper towel–draped plate, she shrugged. "I didn't expect us to be best buddies right off the bat." That wasn't exactly true. She had hoped they'd form a bond quickly. Reality just didn't work out that way.

"Good. At least you're keeping realistic expectations." His stare burned her back. "Can I help you with anything?"

She moved the grease pan to the back burner. "No, thank you. I've got it under control." As soon as she said the words, she realized she hadn't even offered him something to drink. Where were her manners? She turned and faced him.

The envelope lay beside his left hand. Her heart sped. "C-Can I get you a glass of iced tea?"

"I'd really prefer a glass of water, if I might impose?"

"Of course." She pulled a glass from the cabinet and hesitated at the freezer. "Would you like ice?"

"Please." He seemed entirely too comfortable in her kitchen. And right beside that hideous envelope.

She filled the glass with ice and water, then handed it to him. His fingers accidentally grazed against hers.

The familiar sizzle was there. She jerked her hand free and busied herself with mixing the sauce for the po'boys.

She grabbed the envelope and slipped it into a drawer. If Jon noticed anything odd, he didn't comment.

"I hear music. Guess Caleb's in his room?"

"Yes. He likes to unwind with music."

"Apparently."

Was that normal for a teenage boy? She opened the French bread and placed it on the cooking sheet. "Would you like to stay for supper?"

He flashed that annoyingly crooked smile. "I'd enjoy that very much."

Great. Southern hospitality had bit her in the behind. Why'd she have to invite him to stay? His magnetism made her nervous enough with just the two of them. How tense would it be when Caleb joined them? Would her brother mention the letter? Panic choked her. She'd have to warn Caleb to keep mum about the blackmail.

She slid the bread into the oven and set the broiler on low and then set the lettuce on the drain board to chop.

"How're you doing? Handling being a single parent to a teenage boy?"

She nearly sliced her finger. Taking a deep breath, she fought to appear nonchalant. "It's an adjustment, as I said."

"I can imagine. Used to living alone...having Caleb forced on you has to be quite a change."

She met his gaze. "He wasn't forced on me. I agreed to be his guardian, yes?"

"Right."

"Why are you here?" Caleb interrupted from the doorway.

The knife clattered to the counter. Sadie's nerves were tangled more than fishing line on a messed-up rod. "Caleb. Um, you remember Mr. Garrison?"

"Yeah." He moved to the fridge and pulled out a soft drink.

"How was school today, Caleb?" Jon asked, apparently not fazed by Caleb's rudeness.

"School."

Oh, this so wasn't going well. Sadie handed the bowl of tossed salad to her brother. "Could you put this on the table, please?"

He met her stare.

God, please let him know to keep his mouth shut about the letter.

Caleb took the bowl without a word and set it on the kitchen table. The thud echoed off the tension in the room. Nothing she could do about the basic stress she and Caleb were under, but what could Jon be thinking?

"So, do you think you'll like your classes?" Jon kept after Caleb.

"Dude, it's summer school." He jerked one of the chairs out from the table. It scraped against the worn linoleum, sending goose bumps racing over Sadie's skin.

"Which you have to attend and pass to qualify as a senior in the upcoming school semester." Jon moved to sit at the table across from Caleb.

Sadie pulled the bread from the oven. "He attended them today." Why couldn't Jon just cut Caleb a little slack? This was only his third day here.

"So he did." Jon sipped his water.

She made three plates, then carried them to the table. She had no choice but to sit between the guys. Po'boys with a side of testosterone, lucky her. She asked them to bow their heads, offered up a short prayer and then spooned salad onto her plate.

A long silence ensued. She wanted to think because they were enjoying the meal, but she knew the truth. So did Jon.

She wasn't fooling anybody. Caleb barely tolerated being in the room.

"This is really good, Sadie." Jon wiped his mouth on the paper napkin.

"Thank you."

"Isn't it, Caleb?" Jon pressed.

"Yes."

Her heart pounded so loudly she was sure Jon could hear it.

In record time, Caleb inhaled his sandwich, scooted his chair back and carried his plate to the sink. He left the kitchen without another word. No "thank you," no "I appreciate it," nothing. Minutes later, music boomed from his room, louder than before.

Jon studied her. "Is that how he always is?"

She stood and carried her glass and plate to the sink. "I told you, we're adjusting."

"Adjustment is no excuse for rudeness." He set his plate in the sink beside hers. "Thank you for a delicious dinner."

Her heart pounded a faster beat than Caleb's music. "Supper," she all but whispered.

"Huh?"

"The last meal of the day is supper, not dinner."

"I see." He smiled and continued to hold her stare. "Would you like me to help you load the dishwasher?"

"No. No, thank you." She needed him to leave. Now. So she could concentrate on the blackmail letter. Decide what she was going to do.

"Okay. I think I'll go talk to Caleb now."

She wanted to tell him not to, to just leave her brother alone, but knew she couldn't. This was his job, why he was here. She nodded and turned to the dishes.

What would Caleb tell him out of her earshot?

Please, Lord, don't let him mention the letter.

FIVE

Sadie Thompson baffled him.

Jon reviewed what Lisa had told him about her. Promiscuous and a drinker—a personality much like Aunt Torey's. It nearly sickened Jon. Recently Sadie appeared to have turned over a new leaf and seemed determined to set her life right. Yeah, right. In his experience, once a person was hooked into a pattern of a certain destructive behavior, it took a major life event to get him or her to change—like a smoker diagnosed with cancer finally kicking the habit.

What had been Sadie's defining moment? If only his heart didn't jump whenever he saw her...if only her eyes didn't twist his insides into knots. Curiosity fanned in his chest, but right now, he had a job to do, a report to fill out, a little delinquent to monitor.

He stopped outside Caleb's bedroom and knocked. No answer. Only ear-piercing music belted from inside. Jon knocked again, then pushed the door open.

The boy-man lay on his back on the bed, eyes closed but hands holding imaginary drumsticks and playing an invisible drum.

"Caleb, I need to talk to you."

His eyes shot open. "What?"

Crossing the room, Jon flipped off the stereo. "I need to talk to you."

"Why'd you do that?" Caleb shifted into a sitting position.

"Because we need to talk."

"So, talk."

Jon gritted his teeth, but leaned against the edge of the dresser in desperate need of refinishing. "I need to know how things are going with you. How you feel about school. How you're getting along with your sister."

"School is school. I showed up, right?"

"How do you feel about it?"

Caleb snorted. "I get my therapy appointment every week, dude. You don't have to worry about how I *feel* about school. Gee, I feel all warm and fuzzy about the place. Great opportunities." He shook his head and grunted. "Is that what you wanna hear?"

"Can the sarcasm." Jon rested his palm on the cracked dresser. "Are you settling in okay here?"

"It's a room and groceries."

Jon gave a quick glance around the space. "Seems like more than that. Stereo, television, computer…looks like you've got quite a setup here." Very costly. How was Sadie affording all this? Her financial report didn't reflect a debt ratio that would allow such expenses.

"It's okay, man. Better than juvie."

That had to be the truth. Jon nodded toward the computer. "Not doing any illegal downloads, are you?"

"Do you think I'm stupid, dude?"

No, but Jon couldn't take any chances. "You know I have the right to check your system at any time, right? To make sure you aren't in violation of your terms of release."

Caleb waved a hand toward the PC. "Knock yourself out."

If the kid did any pirating, he probably hid it well. Jon wasn't that adept at computers. He decided to try another angle. "How about living with your sister? How are you two getting along?"

Caleb shrugged. "She's here."

"That's it? She takes you in, feeds you, provides all this for you and all you can say is *she's here?*" With the money spent on the electronics around the room, Sadie could've bought a new living room set, which she clearly needed. It was obvious she was trying and Caleb was resisting.

"What do you want me to say? She's doing all this because she has to. Probably getting a kickback from the state so they don't have to take me in."

Jon straightened and advanced on the kid. He bent until he was eye to eye with Caleb. "Listen to me and listen good. You think you know everything? Let me tell you something, you don't know a thing. If it wasn't for your sister, you'd be in the system and no telling what could happen to you. She didn't *have* to take you in, but she did. And she gets no compensation for being your guardian." He straightened. "Got that?"

"Yeah." But the teen's eyes blinked with fear Jon hadn't seen in a long time.

"And you'd better take your classes very seriously. You're on notice, *dude*. One slipup, and you're back in juvie so fast it'll make your head swim. Got that?"

"Yeah."

Jon stared at Caleb, wondering what could be going on in that thick head of his. It was apparent the boy had already made his choice to continue on his trek down the wrong path in life. Shame, because the kid was smart, maybe too smart. And having Sadie as a guardian…well, the chances of Caleb being able to get his life back in line were slim to none. Nothing more for Jon to do but keep tabs on him until his probation was over, then he'd have to release him. And Caleb would most likely end up in prison within a year, if he even made it off probation without incident. "I'll expect you in my office for your appointment later this week."

"Whatever."

Jon paused at the door. He had to give it one more try. "You know, Caleb, you'd better get your act together. I can have you sent back today."

"Threatening me?"

"Promising."

Jon shut the door behind him. The music blasted immediately. He took a deep breath, held it for a moment, then released it slowly. The kid wouldn't listen.

Caleb Frost was a lost cause, even if it weren't for Sadie's unsteady influence.

He shouldn't care how she felt, what happened to her, how Caleb's attitude had to hurt her. No, he shouldn't care even one iota about Sadie Thompson's emotions.

But he did.

"Can I talk to you for a minute?"

Sadie glanced up from her list of suspects to meet her brother's inquiring look. She'd finished cleaning the kitchen, seen Jon out and had changed into shorts and a T-shirt. Now she sat curled up in the recliner in the living room, reading the names until she thought she'd go blind. She smiled. "Sure." Her heart leaped. Would Caleb finally accept the olive branch she'd offered?

He sat on the arm of the couch, his long legs spread out in front of him. "I'm sorry if I've seemed rude to you."

Tears burned the backs of her eyes. "It's okay. We're adjusting."

"No, I've been really rude to you and you don't deserve that."

"Okay." She chewed the inside of her lip, not sure what else to offer. She didn't want to close the door on the conversation, but didn't know how to proceed, either.

"I thought you'd taken me in because you had to." He lifted his gaze from the floor, meeting her eyes.

"No, I wa—" Well, she hadn't exactly *wanted* to take him in. "I couldn't let you become a ward of the state." She let out a sigh. "After Mom died, I had to live in a foster home for a couple of months. It was awful." She shuddered, blinking to ban the memories. "You're my brother, Caleb, even though we really don't know each other very well."

"Well, thanks. I *do* appreciate it." He shoved to his feet. "And I don't know anything about that letter you got, but I'll find out what's going on."

She stood, as well. "No, Caleb. Let me handle it." She gestured to the paper on the chair. "I'm working through possible suspects. I'll figure out who has the biggest beef against Vermilion Oil."

Caleb snorted. "What're you gonna do then? Take the name to the police?" His hands fisted at his sides. "I won't go back to juvie and that's just what they'll do first thing."

Sadie took a step back. The force of her brother's words stung, as well as the logic behind them. "I won't go to the police. But, Caleb, I have to do something."

"I told you, I'll find out what's going on."

"No, it's dangerous and you should stay out of it." Maybe it hadn't been such a wise decision to show him the stupid letter.

He scowled. "I'll be eighteen in a few months. I think I can handle this. They're using me to blackmail you." He headed for the foyer. "I'll be back in a couple of hours. I need to think." He opened the door.

"Caleb, wait!"

"Don't worry. I'll be back by ten." The door clicked shut behind him.

He shouldn't be out alone, but it wasn't as if he was under house arrest. She couldn't treat him like a child, but he *was* her responsibility. Sadie paced the worn rug in the living room, visions of multiple horrors streaming through her head. What if the blackmailers were watching them? What if they followed Caleb, hurt him? Should she go after him?

Lord, how do I take care of him, keep him safe? I don't want him to think I consider him a child, but someone threatened him.

Sadie marched into the kitchen, searching for her purse. She couldn't let Caleb go out alone. Not like this. Not knowing who the blackmailers were or what they wanted.

Brrringgg! Brrringgg! Brrringgg!

She jumped at the sound, then grabbed the cordless phone from the counter. "Hello?"

"Sadie, another facility's been sabotaged. And this time, it's bad. Barrels of oil and saltwater have gone into the bayou." Deacon's voice trembled with emotion. "I need you at the office now."

Oh, no! The situation couldn't be any worse. She should've gone over that list of laid-off workers closer. What was she supposed to do now? Work or Caleb? Both were her responsibilities, but she couldn't be in two places at once. "I ca—"

"Sadie, I really need you here. The Coast Guard's been called in and the press is already at the front door."

Lord, what do I do?

She didn't have a choice—she had a job to do and right now, that had to take precedence. If she failed, she could lose her job and then how would she support Caleb? "I'm on my way."

She hung up the phone and raced to her bedroom. She traded the shorts for a pair of slacks, the T-shirt for a blouse and slipped on a pair of flats. After pulling her hair into a loose bun, Sadie scrawled out a quick note to Caleb to let him know what had happened.

Maybe she'd pass him on her way out.

She whispered a prayer for God to watch over her brother as she turned the key in the ignition.

The evening air had only cooled a few degrees. Sadie flipped on the air-conditioning in her old car and steered toward Vermilion Oil. Her mind sorted through what Deacon had told her while she used her cell to call her assistant. If it was as bad as Deacon said, they'd need all hands on deck for damage control.

"Hello?"

"It's me. I need you at the office pronto."

"Another facility?"

"Yep, and according to Deacon, this one's leaked into the bayou."

"Oh, rats."

"Right. I'm on my way now."

"Meet you there."

Sadie tossed her cell back into her purse, but her mind wouldn't stop tripping over questions. Who could be sabotaging the facilities? And why? Was it really one of the men who'd been laid off? She'd have to get through her suspect list faster. She hadn't been able to speak to the investigator Deacon had hired, and she still had twenty-one names to muddle through.

She didn't pass her brother on the short drive to the office, which bore even more questions to harass Sadie— Where was Caleb? Was he safe?

She parked in the back lot to avoid the press Deacon had warned her about. She couldn't make a statement until she had the most up-to-date information. Sadie slammed the car door and bounded up the back stairs of the office. A group of locals marched around the back parking lot, signs with Get Out of Our Bayou sparkling under the security lights. Could they be so desperate to have the rigs removed from their hunting and fishing grounds that they'd sabotage the facilities? Sadie ignored their shouts as she unlocked the door and slipped inside.

A rush of cool air splayed against her face as she entered the building. Her footsteps echoed off the walls. She'd barely made it down the hallway before voices reached her.

"Sadie, thank goodness you're here. Deacon's a mess." Candy-Jo, Deacon's wife, stood wobbly in the breakroom, holding two cups of coffee.

"Where is he?"

"In the conference area. Sheriff Theriot's here, as well as a guy from the Department of Environmental Quality. The representative from the state's Department of Natural Resources is on his way. Deacon's fit to be tied."

Great. The alphabet-soupers. Sadie quickened her steps as she marched to the conference room. She sucked in a deep breath, fighting to appear calm and collected. She steadied herself and rounded the corner. "Good evening. Sorry I'm a little late."

Relief flooded Deacon's face before he turned to the men. "Sheriff Theriot, I believe you know Ms. Thompson." He nodded at the suit sitting at the conference table. "Mr. Morris, this is my public relations manager, Sadie Thompson."

"Gentlemen." She nodded, grabbed a legal pad and pen from the desk and took a seat. "What's the status?"

"The status, Ms. Thompson, is that one of Vermilion Oil's facilities has leaked approximately four hundred barrels of crude oil and saltwater into the bayou." Mr. Morris shoved his wire-rimmed glasses back up his nose. "But that's just an estimate. The Coast Guard is on its way as we speak and they'll be able to give us a more accurate amount."

Sadie did the math in her head. Four hundred barrels…the spill would take months and millions to clean up. Would this put Deacon in bankruptcy? No, she'd file immediately for federal grants to help in the cost of cleanup. But it would cost Deacon, and not just money.

"We don't know the extent of the leak just yet." Deacon's voice cracked. "But it was sabotage again. The tank valves."

She nodded, her mind scrambling for what to say. She glanced at Sheriff Theriot. "Let me guess—y'all have no suspects at this time?"

"We're following any and all leads, Ms. Thompson." The sheriff kept his tone as rigid as his posture.

Sure they were. "What about the local group of fishermen and hunters who've been publicly speaking out against Vermilion Oil? They want the company out of their bayou. Surely that's strong enough motive for you to follow up with? A group of them are out back, waving picketing signs."

Sheriff Theriot nodded noncommittally. "I said we're following any and all leads. We're looking into them. I'm not at liberty to discuss the investigation with you at this time."

Only problem was that they wouldn't dig deep enough. She'd

have to make sure the leads were followed up. "Well, that's not good enough." Sadie rose, grabbing her notebook. "Something needs to be done immediately." She glanced at her boss.

"This facility is located near a federal wildlife reserve. The federal investigators are on their way." Mr. Morris had such smugness in his words that Sadie tightened her hand into a fist.

Without waiting for anyone to reply, Sadie spun on her heel and marched from the room.

Only when she was safely ensconced behind her desk in her private office did she give in to the emotions and shake profusely.

She was in way over her head. *Oh, Lord, please give me wisdom. I don't know what to do.*

"How can I help?" Georgia breezed into the office, tossing her purse onto Sadie's desk and fisting her hands on her hips. "This is a mess. I passed at least three media vans out front. Not to mention a group of local men and they didn't sound too happy."

Sadie swallowed her groan. "Coffee. Let's start with caffeine."

Georgia rushed from the room. Sadie lifted the phone and punched in her home number. The phone rang four times before her own recorded voice greeted her. She slammed the phone down. Great. Caleb wasn't back yet.

Georgia appeared at her side and set a steaming cup of coffee on the desk. Sadie mouthed her thanks and rubbed her temples. "What in the world is going on?"

"I don't know, but we can't wait for the sheriff to figure it out." Sadie pinched the bridge of her nose. "Can you get me a list of all the local fishermen and hunters who've protested against us? About five of them are in the back parking lot, yelling. It's time we start digging into their motives."

"You got it." Georgia let out a heavy sigh. "What else can I do?"

Lifting her head, Sadie smiled at her assistant. "You can prepare a brief statement to release to those goons out front."

"Stating what, exactly?"

Sadie glanced out her window into the bayou's darkness—would the night ever end? "Just state that we're in the twelfth and final round, have gone down for the count and can't be saved by the bell."

SIX

Dirty-blond hair...wide, emotional eyes hiding...fear?

Jon groaned and slipped on his sunglasses. Sadie Thompson filled his waking thoughts, just as she'd haunted his dreams last night. The morning sun crested over Lagniappe, tossing prisms of light through the cypress trees lining the road. Jon squinted against the glare on the windshield as he turned into the parking lot of the office. Barely eight on a Thursday morning, and he was already distracted. All thanks to his mind not being willing to relinquish the images of Sadie.

Dinner—no, supper—with her had been interesting. He sensed a vulnerability in her, even though she fought to hide it well. It was her quiet susceptibility that caused a gut reaction in him. Had to be. Couldn't be that he was actually attracted to her. No, no way. Women with a reputation like hers were a complication to be avoided. She reminded him too much of Aunt Torey. He would put Sadie Thompson right out of his mind, totally and completely.

But as he strode into the building, Jon couldn't help but recall how nervous she'd been around him last night. Because of Caleb's attitude? No, he'd detected something else. Something more. Jon didn't know what, but his gut instinct told him she'd been hiding something from him. He'd always been a sucker for a mystery.

And Sadie Thompson was an enigma.

"Morning, Lisa." Jon kept his fast stride as he passed her desk.

He had a pile of paperwork awaiting him because he'd had appointments all day yesterday.

Good, paperwork. Nothing like a mound of reports to process to keep his mind on work where it should be, not on some woman with killer eyes and a sad smile.

Sitting down, he booted up his computer and grabbed his case files. Reports had to be made and sent in to the home office or he'd get a nasty letter.

He spied the top folder and groaned. Caleb Frost. The initial interview and first home visit report needed to be completed and mailed in to the state. Jon scanned his notes, tapping a pen against the desk. In his professional opinion, Caleb didn't stand a chance of rehabilitation, and that's what he'd put in his report. He'd seen similar situations way too often and the success rate was below twenty percent. It was his job to use such percentages in his reports. He suspected Sadie wouldn't be too happy with his findings. He told himself he wouldn't care about what she'd think when she got her copy of the report.

Yet deep inside, he did care. Too much, if he was honest with himself.

His intercom buzzed, yanking him from his errant thoughts. Lisa's voice floated through the line. "Lance Wynn on line two for you."

He reached for the phone. "Jon Garrison."

"Hi, Mr. Garrison. It's Lance Wynn."

"What can I do for you, Lance?"

"I need to reschedule my appointment for tomorrow. Your secretary said I'd have to talk to you."

Lisa probably wouldn't appreciate being referred to as a secretary, but that was beside the point. "Why do you need to reschedule?"

"In case you haven't caught the news, my family's going through a lot right now. I need to help my father's company."

Jon brought up Lance's file on the computer. "Yeah, I heard about that. Nasty stuff, the sabotage. And the murder at the rig."

"It is. And last night, another one was sabotaged. This one's leaked stuff into the bayou. So you can see why I need to reschedule my appointment with you."

Jon scanned the notes on the computer. "So, you and your father are working together?" According to the last entry, Lance and Deacon Wynn still weren't on good terms. Had the trials of the company brought father and son back together?

Lance paused. "I'm trying. I think if I can help my dad get through this, we'll be okay. I need to prove to him that I care."

Sounded more like wishful thinking on Lance's part to Jon, but he had to admire the young man for trying to get back in his father's good graces. Then again, with millions of dollars at stake, who could blame Lance for going all-out in his attempts? Jon scrolled down his notes. "What about your relationship with your stepmother? How's that going?"

"We basically avoid each other."

Not as much progress there, but then again, Lance hadn't referred to the new Mrs. Wynn in his usual derogatory manner, so that counted for something. "We talked about your acceptance of her, remember?"

"I'm working on that. I just know she's nothing but a gold digger, ready to bleed my father dry."

"And you also know the choice is your father's, not yours. He's a grown man and has to live with any decisions he makes."

"I realize that. I told you I'm working on it, but right now, we have to focus on the problems at the company. That's where I *can* help my father."

Jon sighed and typed in notes on the computer. "Okay. Come see me Monday morning at nine."

"Thanks, Mr. Garrison."

Jon replaced the receiver, closed the computer file and glanced at the case folder open on his desk. At least Lance was trying to rebuild his life, mend his damaged relationship with his father, no matter his reason.

Which was more than he could say for Caleb Frost.

* * *

She looked like a day-old gar that'd washed up from the bayou.

Sadie stared at her reflection in the mirror, taking in her bloodshot, puffy eyes and pallor. Some signs of stress and sleep deprivation, makeup just couldn't hide. She made a face at herself and tossed the powder brush into the basket on the bathroom counter before moving to the kitchen.

Pouring herself another cup of coffee, she glanced out the window. Caleb stood at the curb, waiting for the bus with two other neighborhood high-schoolers who attended the summer session. She tried to ignore the pain over Caleb's mood this morning. She'd questioned him about his outing last night, but he'd been nothing but evasive. Honestly, she hadn't had the energy to keep trying to get details out of him. A root canal sounded more appealing. Besides, she had more suspects she needed to check into.

The other boys horsed around while Caleb bobbed his head to the music from his earbuds. The summer school minibus turned the corner. Sadie lifted her cup for another sip, but froze as her heart jumped into her throat.

One of the boys shoved the other into the road, just as a car gunned the engine to pass before the flashing lights danced on top of the bus. In a flash, Caleb grabbed the boy by his backpack and jerked him free from the path of the car, tossing him to the ground just as the bus skidded to a stop.

Thank You, Jesus!

She nearly dropped her cup, ready to bolt out the door and check on Caleb. But her brother gave a hand up to the boy now flat on his back in the grass. Together, the three boys crossed the street to clamber onto the bus.

Tears welled in her eyes. Caleb had just saved that kid's life. He'd thought quick and acted faster. Amazing. Despite his attitude around her, Caleb had a good heart. Sadie turned from the window and clicked off the coffeepot. She'd known her brother had some good in him. This was proof.

With a smile on her face, Sadie gathered her purse and brief-case. Even though work would be a beast today with the media, Deacon and her own exhaustion, Sadie was filled with happiness. Deep inside, Caleb had grown into a young man of integrity. She'd just have to break down his barriers where their relation-ship was concerned. Hope widened her smile. They would make this sibling relationship work. It would just take a little more time for him to learn to trust her.

Buzzzzzzzzzzz!

She started. Who could be ringing her doorbell? She shouldn't even be home this late in the morning, but Deacon had said she could come in late. She'd stayed at the office until nearly midnight last night on the phone with the major networks in New York and the company's lawyers, fighting to do as much damage control as she could. On top of that, she'd gone over every single per-sonnel file of the workers who were laid off. She'd verified alibis, confirmed those who had moved away, and now had a list of five men who'd risen to the top of her suspect list. She'd also filed the form online for the federal grant application. If Deacon could get some help with the cost of cleanup, maybe he'd be able to hang on. The long hours and stress explained her atrocious appearance this midmorning.

Buzzzzzzzz!

"I'm coming." Sadie rushed down the hall, smoothing her blouse as she did. She gripped the knob and flung open the front door.

Nobody.

She stepped onto the porch, looking up and down the side-walk along the road. Nary a person in sight. Odd, very odd. She turned to go back inside when she spied a white envelope on the rug in front of the door.

An envelope with her name written in bold, black, block letters.

Bile rose into the back of her throat. She snatched the envelope, glancing over her shoulder. Still no one in sight.

Sadie hurried back into the house, slamming the door behind her. Her hands trembled as she turned the dead bolt. With her back against the wall, she slid down into a crumpled heap on the floor, clutching the envelope.

No chance they'd forgotten about her. Her heart pounded against her ribs. She pinched the bridge of her nose, struggling to regulate her breathing.

Better to get it over with than prolong the agony.

She slit open the envelope and pulled out the paper. Her heartbeat escalated as she read.

BACK OFF YOUR INVESTIGATION INTO THE DAMAGE HAPPENING AT VERMILION OIL IMME-DIATELY, OR YOUR BROTHER'S BODY WILL BE FOUND IN THE BAYOU. DON'T GO TO THE POLICE. WE ARE WATCHING YOU.

She let the letter drift to the floor. She couldn't do this alone. Not anymore. But who to turn to?

Not the police. No, she'd been hassled by them too often in her past. And Caleb was right—they'd probably pull him into child protective services and send him to a foster home. Besides, the letter told her not to go to the police. And it also said they were watching her.

Shivers rippled over her body.

But if she didn't go to the police what would happen to Caleb?

Tears escaped down her cheeks. Just when happiness and hope had bloomed, this letter had to come and drown them out with fear and loathing.

She needed someone she could talk to, someone who was official, but not in law enforcement—just in case someone tried to take Caleb from her. Who would believe her? She couldn't involve Pastor Bertrand—he and his family had been through enough in the past several months. She couldn't talk to Georgia—how could she involve her friend?

Jon Garrison's image flitted across her befuddled mind. Could he help her? He had resources. He had to protect

Caleb, right? Would he honor the demand and not go to the police? Was she confusing her own personal feelings toward him with his position?

Was she willing to take that chance?

"You got the report from Terrebonne juvie." Lisa smiled at him from the doorway of his office. "Pretty fast, considering. It just came by FedEx."

"FedEx, huh? And the state won't let me use anything but the good ol' United States Postal Service." Jon shook his head and took the envelope from Lisa. "Thanks."

"No problem." She hesitated at the door. "I'm going to lunch. Want me to pick you up anything?"

"No, thanks. I'll grab something later."

She shrugged and left without further conversation.

Jon ripped open the envelope and withdrew a folder. He'd only tossed the packaging into the trash when his outer office door slammed.

"Mr. Garrison?"

He stood and moved from behind his desk.

Sheriff Theriot and two men in suits lumbered in the doorway.

"May I help you?"

The sheriff gestured to the men. "These are Special Agents Ward and Lockwood with the FBI."

He nodded at the men. "The FBI? To what do I owe the honor?"

Agent Ward had a large bald spot that glistened under the low-wattage overhead lights. "We need a list of all parolees and those on probation in the area with a history of violence. Also, any who ever worked for Vermilion Oil."

"And any who make their living fishing or hunting in the swamp." Agent Lockwood wore a trimmed goatee that made Jon think of those clichéd villains in silent films.

"May I ask for what?"

"We're looking for suspects who could be involved with the sabotages of Vermilion Oil's facilities," Agent Ward replied.

Ah, grasping at straws because they had nothing. "Why is the FBI involved? Seems more like state agencies would be handling the investigation."

"The contaminants that were leaked into the bayou in last night's sabotage have spread to a federal wildlife reserve." Agent Lockwood squared his shoulders. "That makes it our jurisdiction."

Jon nodded and slipped behind his desk. He logged in to his active database, highlighted and printed those sorted by violent crimes. He did the same thing with those who worked at, or had worked for, Vermilion Oil. The printer hummed as the papers fed through the feeder. "There are about twenty names on each of these lists."

"We'll cross-reference them with the evidence we have." Lockwood spoke to Ward, ignoring Jon and the sheriff. Arrogance seeped from his every pore.

Jon took the papers and handed them to the sheriff. "Here you go."

Agent Lockwood intercepted, almost yanking them from Sheriff Theriot's grasp. He narrowed his eyes at Jon before turning and striding from the office. Agent Ward followed silently.

"You're welcome," Jon said to their retreating backs.

"I'm sorry about that." The sheriff held his hat in his hands. "Not your fault."

Sheriff Theriot chuckled. "Thanks for understanding. Appreciate your getting that so quickly for them."

"I learned my lesson long ago to just do what the men in black ask. A lot less aggravation that way."

"Amen to that." The sheriff moved to go. "Thanks again."

Jon returned to his desk and reprinted the lists he'd given the agents. Which one were the FBI about to focus on?

And what could he do about it?

SEVEN

Desperation guided Sadie's drive to Vermilion Parish Fellowship, Spencer Bertrand's church, despite her resolve not to involve him. She just knew she needed to find some peace.

Her life had been sucked into hurricane-strength velocity and she needed something to cling on to. Some form of peace and direction. Blackmail, work, Caleb...how was she to cope with the enormity of it all?

She couldn't, which was why the shelter she'd found last year in Jesus beckoned to her as she left Lagniappe's city limits.

But Sadie couldn't stay long—she had the afternoon appointment with the group of fishermen. Deacon expected her to put out all the media fires, including the outcry of these men, but she had something else in mind. The timing of it all struck her as suspicious—the wells went up in the bayou, these men complained with a vengeance, then the sabotages began. Maybe she could ferret out something in her meeting with them. Of course, now they had a legitimate reason to be outraged—the leaking of contaminants into the bayou would directly affect their income and way of life. Would they have stooped so low as to damage the facility for the sake of proving their claims about the danger they represented?

But on the other hand, she'd called the investigators recommended by the company's lawyers and turned over her suspect list of five laid-off workers to them. She'd also given them the names of the nature-loving protestors Georgia had compiled. So many people had motive to sabotage the facilities. So many people, individually or as a group, could be the guilty parties.

Which group were the blackmailers aligned with?

Sadie parked in the loose gravel lot outside the church. Oppressive heat and humidity cloaked the air. Her legs felt sluggish, as if stuck in the swamp, as she climbed the rickety stairs and entered the sanctuary. Gentle coolness encapsulated her immediately. She barely made it to the last pew before collapsing. Tears of despondency washed her face.

"Sadie, what's wrong?" Pastor Spence's words were as comforting as his hand on her shoulder.

She swiped the tears away. "I can't take it anymore. Work's gone beyond bad, having Caleb isn't at all like I expected, his probation officer thinks I'm an unfit guardian and…and, well, there's so much emotional stuff to deal with right now." Her body trembled.

"Life can seem overwhelming. Let me ask you this, how do you normally deal with stress?" Spence lowered himself beside her on the pew.

"A year ago, I'd have gone to the club, had a few too many drinks and found somebody to party with to forget all about the stress." She sniffed and offered a shaky smile. "I can't do that anymore."

He returned the smile. "No, you can't. But you already know that." A somber expression covered his face. "Have you prayed about all this?"

"Yes and no." She shrugged. "I just assumed that it'd get easier."

"What would get easier?"

"You know, everything. Once I gave my life to Christ, I knew I'd still have bad times, but not like this."

"What do you mean?"

Where to start? "Well…" How could she explain without going into detail? Start with the most minor infraction. She cleared her throat. "Caleb's probation officer thinks I'm an unfit guardian because of my past."

Spence's eyes widened. "He came right out and said that?"

"No, but the way he questions me…stares at me, I know." Her voice cracked with emotion. "He knows about my past and doesn't approve. Probably thinks Caleb would be better off in a foster home. How do I deal with that? The whispers, the innuendos? I've worked so hard to change, to prove to these people I'm not that person anymore."

"You can't control what others think, Sadie. All you can do is pray for them. Father will deal with them in His way, in His time, just like He did with you."

"But it hurts so much." Fresh tears burned her eyes.

"I know." Spence touched her shoulder again. "You've been handling the gossip and talk for several months without it really getting to you. Why's it upsetting you so much now?"

She hesitated, not knowing how to answer the question. Why was she so upset? Why were Jon's assumptions so different from everyone else's? "Well, because if I'm determined to be an unfit guardian, Caleb will become a ward of the state, and I refuse to let that happen."

"It takes more than a colored past to prove you are an unfit guardian, Sadie. I'd also suggest you talk with Caleb's probation officer. It's my experience that they really do try to make things work."

But Caleb being in danger and her not being able to protect him would throw him right into the state's waiting arms. Maybe she should tell Jon and let the state take custody of him—at least then he'd be safe. She recalled the foster home where she'd been placed. If the foster homes now were anything like what she'd experienced, Caleb wouldn't be safe as a ward of the state. She took another deep breath. "And it's hard because we aren't as close as I'd like."

Spence chuckled. "Typical teenage guy. On top of that, there's no telling what he was exposed to under his father's influence or even in the detention center."

"True, but I'm trying to help him."

"Give him time, he'll come around."

"Are you sure about that?"

"Have you turned it over to God?"

"I think so."

"If you've given the situation to Him, stop trying to take it back. Not seeing immediate results doesn't mean He isn't working on the situation."

"I know all that, I do, but sometimes…"

"Lean on your faith, Sadie. He brought you to it, so He'll see you through it. Not to say it'll be easy, there are no guarantees of that, but He won't leave you to go through it alone."

And she knew Pastor was right. She had to trust God. But it was so hard… "And work's all a mess."

"I caught your press conference. I'm so sorry everything seems to be happening to you at once. Is there anything I can do to help you? You know I'm praying for you."

"Would you pray with me?"

"Of course." He took her hand.

She bowed her head and listened, opening her heart to her Redeemer.

Thirty minutes later found Sadie refreshed and renewed in spirit and pulling into the parking lot of the office. The angry group of locals circled the door. She'd been wrong—the press weren't the vultures, these guys were. Was one of them the black-mailer?

Sadie took a deep breath, fixed a nonpatronizing smile upon her face and headed into the mob. "Good afternoon, gentlemen. If you'll follow me." As she said the words, Sadie turned and led them down the hall to the downstairs conference room.

The men followed, albeit mumbling and grumbling, but at least not shouting. Yet.

She waved at the receptionist, who already had security standing at the ready. Sadie winked at the two burly men as she led the group to the room off the main hallway. She immediately noticed the water pitchers and glasses in the center of the table. At least Georgia was on top of her game. Sadie took a seat at the table, but not at the head. She didn't want them, even subconsciously, to think she perceived herself their superior. No, she wanted them to feel as if they were on a level playing field.

The men filled in the seats around her, the odor of dirt and sweat permeating the room. Sadie poured herself a glass of water and fought to compose herself. Deacon should be here defending himself and his company. These men didn't want to hear her platitudes—they wanted answers directly from the man himself. Yet that's what he paid her to do, so she'd do her very best to remain calm and try to get these men under control.

"Gentlemen, let me first say that the management of Vermilion Oil is completely distraught over the contaminants leaked into the bayou. Every precaution had been made to ensure the wells and facilities would protect the bayou."

"Apparently they didn't work so well," one of the gruff hunters spat out.

"Actually, they did and would have continued to do so had they not been sabotaged." Sadie swallowed against a dry mouth. These men were more than concerned; they were angry. The sad part was she understood they had every right to be.

"Don't matter. If the rigs weren't there in the first place, this leak never woulda happened."

She took another sip of water. "I understand how you feel. But Vermilion Oil's rigs in the bayou produce over twelve hundred barrels of oil each month. That's twelve hundred barrels that's produced in the United States, not in the Middle East."

One of the men slammed his palm on the table. "I don't care where the oil comes from. I do care that now I can't fish for a year because the oil's leaked and the fish will die. What am I supposed to do about money for this year?"

Sweat pooled at the base of her back. How was she supposed to defuse such logical complaints? "Vermilion Oil is working with the Coast Guard and other agencies to enact the fastest and most productive form of cleanup possible. I can assure you that we're taking every conceivable step to quickly remove the contaminants from the waterways."

"And what do you intend to do to prevent it from happening again?" a woman's voice asked from the doorway.

Sadie spun to find a very pregnant CoCo LeBlanc-Trahan striding into the room. CoCo, alligator conservationist. Lover of the bayou. A formidable opponent.

And the bayou was definitely CoCo's forte.

"Sorry I'm late." The dark-haired woman took the seat at the head of the table, smiled at several of the men already seated, then stared at Sadie. "So, what measures is the company taking to ensure another leak doesn't happen?"

Sadie's stomach knotted. Oh, of all the people in Lagniappe to have to face on opposite sides of an issue, why did it have to be her? CoCo had always been devoted to opposing oil and gas rigs in the bayou, clashing with Sadie on a couple of previous occasions. Before she'd been saved, Sadie had made passes, numerous passes, at Luc Trahan. Now Luc was married to CoCo and they were expecting their first child in two months. The dynamics of the situation turned Sadie's stomach. She straightened her shoulders. The bayou might be CoCo's passion, but the boardroom was Sadie's.

"Vermilion Oil is working closely with law enforcement in cooperation with other governing agencies to find these culprits so no future sabotage will occur."

CoCo tilted her head slightly. "Really? All that to say you haven't a clue who's behind these acts, so you have no way of guaranteeing something like this won't happen again to Vermilion's rigs."

"There's no way to guarantee such."

CoCo smiled, sending unease throughout Sadie. "Sure there is. Close down all the wells in the bayou until you catch the guys."

"Mr. Garrison!"

Jon stood from behind his desk. Lisa had already left, so the man's voice surprised him. He stuck his head out of his office door to see the man standing in the room. "Bruce. What are you doing here?"

"I need to talk to you. I have to report something." The man wore a tense expression.

"Sure, come on in." Jon waved the man inside before returning to his desk. "What can I do for you?"

Bruce sat on the edge of the wooden chair in front of the desk. "According to my papers, I'm supposed to report to you any contact I have with the police, right?"

"Right. Let me get your case open." Jon searched for the file on his computer, worried about the man as he read the notes.

Bruce Boudreaux: incarcerated four years for assault on his supervisor who'd just pink-slipped him; time served without incident; sentenced to two years probation and five years supervised release; already served eighteen months of probation with no violations.

"Okay. Have you had a run-in with the police?" Jon studied Bruce, taking in the wideness of his eyes, the paleness of his complexion.

"The FBI. Two agents came with Sheriff Theriot, asking me about those damaged wells."

Oh, no. The feds sure acted fast on this one. "I know. They're just following all leads."

"They came to my place of employment. Asked me where I was on certain days—like I can remember things like that. They told me they'd be checking out my story and coming back." The man's hands shook. "I don't know what they're talking about. I didn't do anything."

Jon knew he couldn't be involved. Bruce was one of the few men on Jon's roster who looked to beat the statistics. He'd gotten married a year ago and his wife expected their first baby in five months. Bruce held down a steady job with a local attorney, doing courthouse records lookups and such.

"Calm down. I'm sure they're just questioning a lot of people right now. You don't have anything to be concerned about."

"I think you're wrong, Mr. Garrison. One of them asked me about my wife's ex-husband working for Vermilion Oil. They said maybe I'd struck out at the company to put him out of work." Bruce stood and paced. "They sounded real serious when they said they'd be back. What am I gonna do? I don't know anything about those damaged wells."

Having met the agents in question, Jon could understand Bruce's distress. But he hadn't known about the wife's connection to the oil company. "Sit down and think carefully."

Bruce plopped onto the chair. "Okay."

"Try to tell me exactly what the agents said."

"Well, I'd just finished work and was heading to my car when Sheriff Theriot came up with these two guys in suits."

Jon nodded.

"The sheriff introduced them as FBI agents. I gotta tell you, I went to sweatin' right then and there. I don't much care for federal agents."

Jon could relate.

"Anyway, they started asking me about my wife's ex-husband. I don't really know the guy, just know he used to knock Allie around when they were married. They seemed real interested in how I felt about my wife's former abuser."

Jon could see exactly where they were going in their line of questioning. "What did you tell them?"

"Just that I thought the guy was a wuss. Any man who'd hit a woman…well, those kind normally won't face someone their own size."

While true, Jon could just imagine what had to run through the agents' minds. "Then what?"

"They started asking me about did I know he worked for Vermilion Oil. I said I knew that. They asked if I knew where he was stationed and I told them I didn't."

Oh, they were setting up all the basics. "What did they say?"

"Wasn't so much what they said, but how they acted. Looked at each other and gave little nods. Kinda like they were going *aha.*"

Yeah, Jon knew exactly what Bruce meant. "What else did they say or ask?"

"One asked me where I was on July fifth and July fourteenth. Before I could answer, the other asked me where I was last night."

The dates of the sabotages. "What did you tell them?"

"The truth. Last night, I was out fishing off Fisherman's Cove."

"And the times before?"

"I couldn't remember. I can't."

Oh, this wasn't good. "Bruce, this is very important. You need to try and remember where you were on the fifth and fourteenth. You need an alibi."

"I know. But I can't remember." Bruce stood and paced again. "I know I need an alibi, but I honestly can't remember. What am I gonna do? What if they come to the house? Upset Allie? You know this pregnancy hasn't been the easiest for her. They'll stress her out."

"I know. Calm down." Jon stood, as well, then perched on the edge of his desk. "Bruce, you need to remember where you were on those nights. Otherwise, they will continue to think of you as a suspect in the sabotages at Vermilion Oil."

A gasp sounded from the doorway. Jon shot his glance there, and his heart hiccuped.

Sadie stood perfectly still, her eyes wide. "Bruce Boudreaux is no more involved in these sabotages than I am."

Jon stood. "Sadie." He glanced at Bruce. "I'm sorry, but this is private—"

She crossed the room to touch Bruce's shoulder. "I know you aren't involved, Bruce. You can't be."

While Jon knew he should escort her from the office, he noticed Bruce didn't look too upset at her presence. "Why do you say that?"

"Because Bruce would never do anything to compromise his and Allie's life." She spoke with such resolve. How could she be so sure?

"I wouldn't. I changed." Bruce's voice was barely above a whisper.

"I know that. I know that people can and do change."

Ah. So that's where the resolve came from. Jon nodded at the door. "I appreciate your input, Sadie, but really, I've got this."

Her eyes narrowed, then she let out a little huff. "Bruce, if you and Allie need anything, you just call me."

"I appreciate that, Sadie."

She didn't bother to say goodbye to Jon as she spun and marched from his office, leaving Jon to assure the shaken and scared Bruce Boudreaux.

EIGHT

The *cooyons!* How could the FBI even entertain the notion that Bruce Boudreaux could be involved with the sabotages?

Sadie had been shocked and appalled by Bruce's dilemma yesterday afternoon. Bruce, along with his sweet wife, Allie, had been among the first to welcome Sadie into the Vermilion Parish Fellowship last year. He was a good Christian man and she no more believed him guilty of sabotage than herself of murdering Jolie Landry. Of course, she'd been accused of exactly that the previous year. The police had caught the guilty party, but it was hardly surprising that she'd been distrustful of the way police jumped to conclusions ever since.

That the FBI had come and harassed the man infuriated Sadie. She knew exactly what it felt like to be an innocent suspect. Her righteous anger drove her so much that she now sat in her car in the parking lot of the grocery store, right down from the sheriff's office. Whether the FBI were working out of the office didn't matter—Sadie determined she'd set the record straight where Bruce was concerned.

DON'T GO TO THE POLICE.

She glanced around the parking lot, looking for anyone out of place. Not that she'd really know. She opened her cell phone and dialed the direct number for the sheriff's office.

The familiar dispatcher, Missy, answered as Sadie identified herself. "Morning, Sadie. How're you this beautiful Friday?" Ever since the woman had gotten engaged to Jayden Pittman, manager of the jazz club, she was downright perky.

Which, today, truly annoyed Sadie. "I need to talk to the sheriff."

"I'm sorry, hon, he's not in right now. He's out with the FBI agents."

Sadie swallowed the scream. "When do you expect him back?"

"Well, now, I don't rightly know. From what I could overhear, they were going to talk to a few people and then meet with some of those government people. You know, the ones crawling over everywhere at your company."

Oh, Sadie knew which ones, all right. "Thanks, Missy." Maybe she'd be able to catch the sheriff and the FBI flunkies at her office. That wasn't exactly going to the police. And surely the blackmailers realized law enforcement would swarm Vermilion Oil because of the sabotages.

She wiped her brow against the smoldering heat—and it wasn't even nine in the morning yet—and steered toward Vermilion Oil. She almost dreaded reporting to Deacon the outcome of her meeting yesterday with the hunters and fishermen. Had it not been for CoCo, she probably could have defused the men. But no...as soon as CoCo had suggested Vermilion Oil shut down all the wells in the bayou until the saboteurs were caught, the men jumped on that and wouldn't quiet down and leave until Sadie had assured them she'd take their suggestion to Mr. Wynn himself. As if he'd do such a thing. He couldn't afford to.

Then again, could he afford *not* to?

Sadie slammed the car door and rushed into the building. A group of men huddled in the corner, whispering and murmuring. She stopped at the receptionist's desk. "What's going on?"

"Those guys are some of the ones Mr. Wynn laid off last month."

"Why are they here?"

"To talk with Mr. Wynn." The young woman lowered her voice. "Security's already on alert."

Sadie glanced over her shoulder at the men. None looked happy. "Does Deacon know they're here?"

The woman nodded. "He said he'd send someone down in a few minutes." Her eyes widened as her gaze lit on the growing-louder-by-the-minute group. "I hope he hurries. They make me nervous."

Understanding, Sadie nodded and moved to the elevators. That group looked as potentially disgruntled as the one she'd faced yesterday. Good thing she didn't have to deal with them. Being railroaded by CoCo had Sadie's self-confidence level down to next to nothing.

She stepped off on the third floor to meet a pacing Georgia. "Girl, where have you been?"

"I had a couple of things to take care of this morning." Sadie inched by her assistant into the office. She tossed her purse and briefcase onto her desk. "What's up?"

"Deacon's been looking for you. Says he has a group of people for you to talk to. And he wants an update from your meeting yesterday with the environmentalists."

Oh, surely not… "This group he wants me to talk to today, they wouldn't happen to be the oil field workers we laid off last month, would they?"

Georgia shrugged. "I don't know who they are. All I know is Deacon is antsy to find you."

As if on cue, Deacon Wynn strode into the office. "There you are, Sadie." He took her gently by the elbow and led her toward the elevators. "I hate to throw a meeting at you last-minute, but those laid-off workers are downstairs, demanding someone talk to them."

"You want me to talk to them? I don't know what to say."

"It's all part of public relations, Sadie." Deacon pressed the down button. "Just tell them something to appease them, anything to shut up their public rants against us."

She pinched the bridge of her nose. "I don't think anything I can say will mollify them, Deacon. They were laid off. How can I justify that?"

"Just repeat what you wrote out for me in that speech I gave when I laid them off."

Was he serious? "Deacon, the main reason we cited for laying men off was because you had invested in the state-of-the-art constant monitoring systems of the facilities to protect the waterway environment."

"Oh."

"For obvious reasons, I can't use the same excuse, yes?" Had he really not remembered what he'd said? This wasn't the Deacon Wynn she knew and respected. The stress must be getting to him even more than she realized.

The elevator door slid open. She stepped in the way so it couldn't close. "They want to hear from you, Deacon. You. As owner of the company. They'll rip me to shreds no matter what I say because they want to hear a Wynn explain."

"Then let me talk with them."

Sadie and Deacon spun around. Lance leaned against the wall. "If they want a Wynn to talk to them, let me do it."

Deacon's face contorted into a grimace. "How'd you get up on this floor?"

"Doesn't matter." Lance pushed off the wall. "Let me help you out here, Dad. Ms. Thompson's right, she can say whatever she wants and it's not gonna be good enough for them."

An angle formed in Sadie's mind. Lance might be the saving grace to the whole situation.

"I've told you—I don't want or need your help."

"Wait a minute, Deacon."

Both boss and son stared at her, questions in their eyes.

"Lance, do you really want to help your father out here?"

"Of course. That's why I'm here."

She turned to Deacon. "If he goes down there and presents himself as part of the managing team, assuring those men we're looking into the situation, as well as considering having the facilities returned to the old method—which would mean re-employment for a good majority of them—that just might be enough to satisfy them for now."

Her boss frowned. "I've invested a lot of money in those self-monitoring facilities."

"And look what's happened." She paused, waiting for Deacon to erupt. When he didn't, she forged on ahead with her idea. "You need to let everyone know the Wynn name stands for something more than making money. That you care about the environment and the parish. That you won't rest until the people responsible for polluting the bayou are punished."

Deacon's eyes lit up brighter than she'd seen in the past month. "So they'll sympathize and support me."

"Yes." She took a deep breath, preparing to lay the bombshell of her idea. "And to further prove your point, have Lance announce that you're shutting down production on all the wells in the bayou until the culprits are found, so that no further contaminants can be leaked."

Her boss shook his head. "I can't do that, Sadie. I'd go bankrupt for sure."

"I've already applied for your grant to assist in cleaning up the bayou and we should hear back on that next week, at the latest. But if you leave the rigs operational in the bayou, you take the chance of them being sabotaged, as well."

"I've beefed up security." Deacon stuck his chest out.

"Which means nothing if another facility is damaged and you have to spend even more in cleanup, even if you do get the grant."

"She's right, Dad."

Deacon bounced his gaze from Sadie to Lance, then back to Sadie. "You think it'll work?"

"I think it'll not only appease the men downstairs, but also the group of environmentalists I spoke with yesterday." She held her breath, waiting to see if he'd go for it. "Those two groups are on top of the suspect lists I handed over to the investigators yesterday. We need to stop these sabotages until the investigators have time to zero in on the guilty party."

Running a hand over his thinning hair, Deacon glared at his son. "Can you say just what Ms. Thompson tells you to say?"

"Of course."

Sadie's heart pounded. Could this be the answer to both her pressing work issues?

"Fine. Do it." Deacon scowled at her. "You cut him off if he veers even a millimeter from what you tell him to say."

"Yes, sir." She motioned for Lance to enter the elevator and followed suit. She pressed the button, tossing a smile at Deacon as the door slid closed.

"Whew. I didn't think he was gonna go for it." Lance finger-combed his hair, using the reflective walls of the car as a mirror.

"Listen, Lance, I only have a minute to brief you. Here's what you need to say…"

Put simply, Sadie was amazing.

Jon stood off to the side, watching Lance address a group of angry laid-off workers with words of grace and hope. Words that were *not* his own. Jon noticed how Sadie stood to Lance's immediate right, every now and again touching his elbow. She'd clearly coached him and coached him well. Lance had never sounded so good.

Jon had stopped by to see Sadie, not knowing Lance would be present. Yet he was grateful he'd been able to see the young man doing what he said he'd be doing—trying to help his father.

Sadie was content to let someone else take the glory of her words. Truth be told, shutting down the wells in the bayou until the crisis had passed was probably her idea, as well. Jon couldn't imagine Deacon Wynn willingly losing money to save the environment. How she'd gotten him to agree to the idea, he couldn't imagine.

She was amazing.

And now he was here to ask for her help. He could've called, but he didn't want to. He wanted to see her. Needed to.

He hated having to ask for anyone's assistance, least of all a woman he couldn't get out of his mind, but he didn't have a choice. She was the one person he believed could actually do something. And for that, he'd swallow his pride, fight his attraction and ask.

Lance ended the meeting with little fanfare, then turned and followed Sadie to the elevators. Jon moved to follow, but the receptionist stopped him. "Sir. Sir, may I ask where you're going?" A burly security guard moved to the counter.

"I'm here to see Sadie Thompson."

"Do you have an appointment?"

"No, but I need to see her. If you'll buzz her, I'm sure she'll tell you it's okay."

"Well, sir, Ms. Thompson's a busy woman."

"I understand that. If you could just call her, please."

"Who are you?" asked a voice from behind him.

He turned to face a petite young woman. "My name's Jon. Jon Garrison."

The woman narrowed her eyes. "And why do you want to see Sadie?"

"It's…" He scrambled for what to say. "Uh, it's personal."

The woman raised a single eyebrow. "Really? Personal, huh?"

"Yes." It'd been a long time since a woman pinned him in place with probing questions. Jon hadn't liked it then and he sure didn't like it now. He refused to give out more information.

"Well, then." She turned to the receptionist. "Call Sadie and tell her a Mr. Garrison is here to see her." She glanced back at Jon before returning her attention to the lady behind the counter. "See what she has to say. We can always have security toss him out if need be."

Oh, great. Wouldn't that just be a hoot? He could see the headlines now— "Probation Officer Escorted Off Private Property." Lisa would probably eat it up.

The receptionist lifted the phone and whispered. The young woman slipped him a sly wink and extended her hand. "Georgia Maldon, Sadie's assistant."

He shook her hand. "Pleasure to meet you."

"Oh, no, the pleasure's mine, I assure you." Why did he get the feeling Georgia enjoyed this encounter on a much deeper level than just on the surface?

The receptionist lowered the phone and stared openly at Jon. "Ms. Thompson will be right down."

Georgia chuckled. "Oh, yeah, the pleasure's definitely all mine."

He had to have missed something, but couldn't think about that right now. All he could do was rehearse in his mind what he'd say to Sadie, how he'd get her to help him. He ignored the woman who looked at him with laughter in her eyes.

The ding sounded mutely across the large area, followed immediately by the clicking of heels against marble floor.

Jon took a deep breath and focused his gaze on Sadie striding toward him.

Her steps were sure and precise, her shoulders squared, her hands tense at her sides. No smile lit her face. "Mr. Garrison, did we have an appointment I forgot?" Apprehension flared in her eyes.

"No, but I was wondering if I could discuss something with you." He cut his eyes to Georgia and then back to Sadie. "In private. Can I interest you in some lunch?"

She, too, glanced at Georgia. "Sure. Let me go get my purse and I'll be right back."

He caught Georgia's too-big grin, but chose to ignore the implication. "I'll pull the car around and pick you up in front of the building."

She nodded before heading off toward the elevator again. He gave a curt nod to Georgia and the receptionist, then rushed back outside. Who ever would've thought stepping back into the humidity and heat would be a welcome relief to the atmosphere inside the air-conditioned building?

He made his way to the car and slipped inside. Sadie had seemed distant a few seconds ago. Did that mean she'd be unwilling to help him? He *really* needed her help.

Jon waited until the hostess sat them at a table off the main room and the waitress had appeared with water, bread and menus before he let out a heavy sigh.

Sadie set the menu aside and tented her hands over the table. "I'm assuming it's not an emergency since we're taking lunch."

"What? Oh, no."

"But it's about Caleb?"

Oh, no. He should've been clearer either at her office or in the car. What horrors must be racing through her mind! "No, this isn't about Caleb. I'm sorry, I should have put your mind at ease earlier."

"If it's not about Caleb, what's this all about?"

The waitress appeared to take their drink orders. Once they'd placed their lunch orders, the waitress scurried off.

Alone again, Sadie held him still with a stare. "What's this about?"

Jon took a deep breath. "I need your help."

NINE

Surprise stole Sadie's voice. Needed her help?

What could she possibly help Jon Garrison with that didn't involve Caleb?

"I don't understand." Her voice cracked as she spoke. "If it doesn't involve Caleb, how can I possibly help you?"

"With Bruce."

She furrowed her brows, thinking. "Bruce Boudreaux? What about him?"

"I understand you attend church with him."

"That's right. Where are you going with this?"

"And you were very adamant yesterday—positive of his innocence."

"Right." She took in his intense expression and her heart skipped. "Don't tell me you think he's involved with the sabotages! There's no way."

"No, I agree with you."

Now she was really confused. "Um, then how do you need my help?"

"To prove his innocence."

She remained silent, waiting for the rest of the explanation.

"You want to know who's really behind the sabotages at your company, right?"

"Yes."

"So help me."

The dots weren't connecting for her, apparently. "I don't understand. Help you what?"

"Well, because I'm sure you're already investigating the sabotages for your business, I'd like to help you investigate to find out who's really guilty, and prove Bruce's innocence at the same time."

Her throat closed up.

BACK OFF OF YOUR INVESTIGATION IMMEDI-ATELY OR YOUR BROTHER'S BODY WILL BE FOUND IN THE BAYOU.

If they investigated together, openly, the blackmailers would know. There was no way she could help Jon, no way at all and keep her brother safe. "I—I—I—"

Jon held his up hands in mock surrender. "Hear me out." He scrubbed his face with his hands. "I know how these federal guys work—they'll concentrate on whomever they think could be guilty, looking for ways to close their case. Sadly enough, in my line of work, I know the truth doesn't always come to light if they're not really looking for it."

"But I was a suspect in a murder case and I wasn't charged."

"Were the feds involved?"

"Well, no, but—"

"I know these guys, Sadie. Not them in particular, but their type. I've seen it time and again. They've got pressure put on them to close a case, get an indictment, then get a conviction. Once they do that, they believe they've done their job. They got their man."

"I can't believe they'd work like that."

The waitress appeared, set their plates in front of them, refilled their tea glasses, then rushed away. The enticing aroma of jambalaya filled her senses, making her stomach growl despite the unsavory conversation.

"Let me bless the food." Sadie bowed her head, not bothering to notice if Jon followed suit or not. She offered up grace, then automatically reached for the salt.

Jon dove right back into the conversation. "It happens all the time. I see it. Some of the people on my probation list never should have been indicted, much less convicted." He took a bite of the steaming lunch special.

No, she didn't want to believe that. But on the other hand, she knew how law enforcement kept coming and coming, grilling and bullying.

"Bruce isn't guilty, but if they make up their collective mind that he is so they can close the case and move on, well…"

Sweet Jesus, what do I do?

Sadie chewed slowly, but couldn't appreciate the Cajun spices flavoring the boudin and rice. She really liked Bruce and his wife and couldn't just sit by and let him be blamed for something she knew he didn't do. But she couldn't risk Caleb's life, either.

What would Jesus do?

Blessed is he who has regard for the weak; the Lord delivers him in times of trouble.

But what about Caleb? Wasn't he innocent, as well?

"Sadie, I really need your help. Bruce needs your help." Jon's voice had turned to pleading.

The image of Bruce filled her mind, followed by his wife's image. Sweet Allie, her tummy just beginning to swell with their first baby.

Speak up and judge fairly; defend the rights of the poor and needy.

Tears that had nothing to do with the cayenne pepper formed in Sadie's eyes. "I could talk to them, as a representative of Vermilion Oil. Maybe make them understand there's no way Bruce is involved."

Jon shook his head and swallowed. "They won't back off. Please, take no offense by this—it isn't my opinion—but they'll write off the opinions of anyone except law enforcement. That's what matters to them."

"Then how can I help you? I'm not in law enforcement by

any stretch of the imagination." She took a quick sip of tea, letting the coolness slide down her throat. Anything for a reprieve from this conversation.

DON'T GO TO THE POLICE.

"You know people here, you have a local angle. They'll open up and talk to you."

Sadie nearly spat her tea across the table. "You're kidding, yes?" She shook her head and let out a snort. "In case you've missed it, I'm not exactly in the people of Lagniappe's good graces." Her past prevented it. As much as that hurt to admit, it was a fact.

"But you're already working on the investigation anyway."

BACK OFF OF YOUR INVESTIGATION IMMEDI-ATELY OR YOUR BROTHER'S BODY WILL BE FOUND IN THE BAYOU.

"I can't get anyone to talk to me," Jon continued. "I'm still called *the Yankee* behind my back."

Her fork clattered to the plate.

"Yes, I hear the whispers. I know that's what they call me. Still. But it hasn't mattered until now, when I need to get info from the locals to prove Bruce's innocence."

"Like they'll talk to me any more openly? I think not."

"But you're PR for Vermilion Oil."

"Which really hasn't needed much except the occasional good community service gig every quarter or so."

"Surely you must have some idea who could be behind the sabotages. Don't you have any suspects?"

Several came to Sadie's mind as she finished off her lunch and dabbed her napkin over her mouth. What was she supposed to do? *Blessed is he who has regard for the weak.*

Bruce was her brother in Christ just as surely as Caleb was her half brother. She couldn't turn her back on either.

Okay, God. I'm going to do this. But I need a lot of help. Please, please keep Caleb safe.

"Anything? Any suspects of your own? Any ideas?" Jon wore the most intense expression.

Sadie studied him, his eyes. Nothing but sincerity blinked back at her from those golden orbs. "Okay, I'll help you. But I have a couple of terms you have to agree to first."

Terms? She had terms before she'd agree to help prove her friend's innocence? Had her outrage just been a show for Bruce's benefit?

Jon twisted the cloth napkin into a ball and dropped it onto his empty plate. "Let's hear your terms."

"I can't publicly come out and help you, or talk too much to law enforcement. I'm, uh, in a delicate situation."

Because of her position with Vermilion Oil?

Her face paled. "There are reasons why I can't be seen out running around investigating, reasons I can't explain to you. Most of what I've been looking into has been done quietly."

He understood. "I don't exactly picture us running around, toting guns and chasing bad guys." He smiled. Somehow, he couldn't picture Sadie in that venue.

She returned the grin. "I meant that I can't be out questioning people right and left, yes?"

Had to be because of her job. Which did put her in a situation, but would also give him more information. Wouldn't the FBI report their findings and leads to the head of the oil company, who surely shared the information with his PR? "I understand."

"You can't tell anyone, not even Bruce, that I'm helping you investigate."

"Gotcha."

"Good." She gave a quick nod. "Then I'll help Bruce in any way I can. Where do we start?"

His mind tripped over ideas. "Well, first things first, do you, as a representative of Vermilion Oil, have any suspects in mind?

Someone who's made a stink about something? I caught your press conference and so forth, so I know there are those out there trying to ruin your company."

Her face went slack. "I have a lot of suspects. Groups, mainly. I'll have to get the names for you. I turned the list over to the police and to the private investigators Vermilion Oil hired." She puckered her lips and bounced her thumbnail off them. "I can get those at the office this afternoon as well as getting an update from the P.I.s."

"Great. I'm going to go talk to Sheriff Theriot. See if I can catch him without the federal goons and get him to talk to me a little bit. As a probation officer, I sometimes can get inside investigation information."

The waitress moved to their table. "Would you like coffee or dessert?" When Jon and Sadie shook their heads, she set the check on the table, thanked them for their business and whisked their lunch plates away.

"Why they would even focus on Bruce is the question."

Jon shrugged. "Because they haven't a clue. Like I said, they're all about convictions, not justice."

"That's so sad. And horrible in this day and age."

"I've seen that the trend of the legal system these days isn't about the truth or justice as much as it is about legal maneuvering. It is sad." And many times, he'd wondered why he stayed employed by the Department of Justice. A decent paycheck? Maybe. He'd chosen his profession because he'd genuinely wanted to help people, thought he could. Now, he'd become too jaded. And who could blame him? Very few of his parolees proved they cared about rehabilitation.

Which made Jon want to fight for Bruce Boudreaux all the more.

"I'd better get back to the office." Sadie reached for her purse. "I'll have names of people I suspect put together this afternoon."

Jon placed two twenties under the check and rose. "And I'll try to catch up with the sheriff and see what I can find out." He put his hand under her elbow as they wove through the tables. Warmth spread up his arm, but he chose to ignore it. He released her to open the restaurant door for her and nearly ran smack into Lisa and a sheriff's deputy.

"Jon! Fancy meeting you here." Lisa laughed.

He glanced at his watch and noticed it was drawing near to two o'clock. How rude of him not to call in to the office. "I didn't realize the time. I'm sorry if you held off your lunch break for me."

"Obviously I didn't, as I'm here." She laughed louder. "I just turned voice mail on and locked the door."

"Oh. Good."

Lisa pulled the man whose hand she held closer. "I've been wanting to introduce y'all. Jon Garrison, this is my fiancé, Mike Fontenot."

Jon took the man's offered hand and shook. "Nice to meet you." He reached for Sadie, drawing her into their circle. "This is Sadie Thompson."

While Mike smiled and said, "We've met. Hey, Sadie," both women just nodded at one another.

Talk about tension.

"Well, I'd better get back to the office and hold the fort." Jon tugged Sadie farther down the walkway. "Nice to meet you, Mike."

"Same to you."

The sun beat down on them as they made their way to his car. He rushed to open the passenger side for her. She shot him a quizzical look before slipping into the seat. Jon quickly moved to his side and started the ignition, turning the air conditioner on full-blast. He put the car in gear and steered toward Sadie's office. "I didn't know Lisa was engaged."

Sadie studied him. "Does that bother you?"

"Oh, no."

"Mike's a nice guy. He used to work at the jazz club."

"Hmm." He turned onto the street housing Sadie's office. "We need to swap info this evening."

"Yes, and set up a plan of action."

He let out a slow breath. "We could meet tonight, for supper."

She jerked her head and stared at him.

"Unless you have a date or something." It hadn't occurred to him that she might have a boyfriend. For some reason, the idea made the jambalaya stir in his gut.

Sadie laughed, full and throaty. "Please. When would I have time for a relationship? With everything going on at work and adjusting to Caleb... No, I'm free tonight."

Relief filled him and he couldn't explain why. Well, he probably could but he'd rather not. "We could go out, if you'd like."

She paused, staring out the windshield as he turned into the parking lot of Vermilion Oil. "No, it'd be better if we're not seen out together all the time. And I don't want to leave Caleb to fend for himself just yet. Why don't you come to the house for supper? I promise to cook something better than po'boys this time." Her laughter lilted.

"Sounds like a plan. What time and what can I bring?" He pulled the car along the curb.

"Six-thirty, and don't worry about bringing anything but information." She opened the door and stepped to the sidewalk. "Thanks for lunch." She shut the car door before he could respond.

He headed back to the office, excited. Not only would he be doing something proactive to help Bruce, but also because he'd get to work closely with Sadie. As if that should make a difference.

Funny thing—it did.

TEN

She'd never get everything done in time.

Sadie rushed about, picking up the place. At least Sunday's newspaper was off the coffee table. Caleb would be home any minute and she needed to tell him about Jon coming over. He probably wouldn't be too happy, but she'd explain and it'd be okay. At least, that's what she prayed.

She finished straightening the living room and moved to the bathroom, which was in dire need of a good cleaning.

After lunch, she'd met with Deacon and updated him, gathered a list of her suspects, checked in with the investigators who had already eliminated more names on her list, then left work a little early. She'd stopped by the store on the way home and picked up three really nice steaks, which were now marinating in the icebox. Friday night and she had a date.

Not a real date. No, she wouldn't even allow her heart to feel hope. This was just a working arrangement. Two people trying to help someone. That was all. She didn't even know if he was a Christian, so it couldn't be a real date. She no longer dated men who hadn't given control of their lives to God. No, it wasn't a real date.

But her heart wouldn't stop pounding at the thought of sharing another meal with Jon Garrison.

The door slammed, rattling the pictures on the wall. Caleb had returned from summer school.

"Hey, Caleb, can you come see for a minute?" She put the toilet brush up and straightened the hand towel on the bathroom rack.

"Yo." He crowded the doorway with his frame.

"Jon Garrison's coming for supper."

"Again?" His slack features twisted into disappointment. "Why's he gotta check up on me so much?"

She emptied the trash can into the bag and replaced it. "Oh, Caleb, he's not here to check up on you."

"Then why's he coming?"

"To see me."

Caleb stepped back as if he'd been slugged. "You two hooking up?"

She should've worded that differently. "No, nothing like that." Heat crept into her face. "We have a mutual friend who needs our help."

"Small town, huh? Everybody knows everybody else."

"I didn't know Jon before you."

Caleb's brows shot up. "So you invited him here?"

"Yes." Sadie leaned against the sink. "Is that a problem?"

Her brother shrugged. "He's the dude who's got me on a leash and you're bringing him around." He shook his head. "Don't make a whole lotta sense to me."

"Our friend is a suspect in the sabotages going on at my work. We both know he's innocent."

"So what's the deal?" Caleb actually looked interested.

"He's a member of my church and on probation. Jon's his probation officer. The FBI seems to have focused their attention on him as the prime suspect."

"I know how it works. Or rather, how it doesn't." He rested his shoulder against the door frame. "Unless you have money."

She hated to hear the cynicism in his voice, but after talking with Jon, she understood his feelings. "Was the FBI involved in your case?" She spoke softly, hesitant to probe too deep and have Caleb retreat back into his silence, but he'd never offered details about what had happened to him.

"Yeah, but they were all right. The judge was the one who was out to get me. Wanted to teach me a lesson, so he gave me a harsher sentence…that kind of thing. But I was in with some guys who weren't so lucky and some who had money got off easy."

Sadie tried to rationalize the logic there, but couldn't. Before lunch with Jon today, she'd have wanted to write off her brother's words as nothing more than that—words. Now, she wondered if they had weight and merit.

Thank You, Jesus, for preparing my mind for Caleb's claims. I'm more open and that will help in our relationship.

Caleb stared at her, as if trying to discern if she would argue the point.

She took a slow breath. "I hate what's become of our justice system."

"You and me both. One guy in juvie, he got busted with crack. Just one point two grams, mind you. That's less than the tip of your fingernail. Got ten years. He's fifteen, so he'll serve three in juvie, then be moved to a fed prison."

Gasping, Sadie covered her hand with her mouth. She'd had no idea.

Caleb seemed to thrive on sharing the horrors. He leaned forward, shoving his hands in his jeans pockets. "Another guy, from here actually, got caught with a stash of pot—with intent to distribute. But all he got was ninety days in juvie, was released the week before he was legal. Dude's family has money, so he'll never serve a day in a real prison. Where's the justice in that?"

"I don't know." She couldn't fathom the lack of balance by the justice system. "But you understand why I want to help my friend, yes?"

"Why?"

"I thought I just explained—"

"No, why would you help this guy? Is he a boyfriend or something?"

She laughed. "Not hardly. He's married and expecting his first baby later this year."

"Then why?"

"Because it's what's right."

"Huh?" He looked as confused as he sounded.

"Caleb, as a Christian, I'm called to help those I can."

"How do ya figure?"

Oh, no. She was still too new in her faith to try her hand at witnessing. *Father God, please give me the words to share. Ones that will reflect Your mercy and grace.* She took a deep breath. "Well, because that's what Jesus tells us in Scripture."

"And you believe that religion stuff?"

"I believe the Bible is the word of God. I believe Jesus is God's son and died for me, for the forgiveness of my sins, yes."

Caleb went silent, but his face grew pensive. "So, what can you do to help this dude?"

At least it was a beginning. She moved past him into the hall. "Give Jon some names of people with an ax to grind against my company. Some groups who I think could be involved."

"You're not gonna work with the police, are you?" Worry sneaked into his voice as he trailed her to the kitchen.

The blackmail.

"Oh, no. I'm working with some P.I.s for the company and will help law enforcement as they contact me, but I'm not working with them at all." Caleb deserved to know about the second letter—he was directly involved. "But I got another note from the blackmailers."

"When?"

Sadie ignored his question and reached for her purse. She passed the letter to him.

His gaze shot back and forth as he read, then he locked gazes with her. "So helping your friend goes against what these dudes are telling you to do?"

Her mouth went dry. Surely he knew she'd protect him, but that she had to do this. Had she explained well enough that it was her duty as a Christian? "I suppose…somewhat."

He smiled. "Cool. Ultimate defiance. I love it."

* * *

Not bad.

Jon stared at his reflection in the rearview mirror a final time. He'd taken more care than usual in dressing for this nondate date. But he knew two facts for sure now:

Sadie Thompson wasn't like Aunt Torey.

And he was attracted to her.

There, he'd admitted it. Now what to do about it was a whole other ballgame.

Letting out a sigh, Jon exited the car and ambled up the walkway to Sadie's porch. He hated that he was so nervous, but there was nothing he could do about it. He knocked on the door.

The door swung open and Jon's mouth went dry. Sadie had changed into a casual pair of calf-length pants with a frilly white shirt and looked as fresh as water to a man in the dessert. "Hey, Jon. Come on in."

When did his tongue decide to not cooperate with his brain? "Thanks." He grinned, hoping to cover his acting like an enamored schoolboy.

The house smelled of flowers and spices, warm and welcoming. Something inside Jon moved into yearning.

"Let's head to the patio. I have the grill going." She moved toward the kitchen door.

Jon followed her, trying desperately to snap out of whatever he'd fallen victim to. Since when did he yearn for anything from Lagniappe? He'd been treated like an outsider since he got here and time hadn't altered that.

Standing over the grill, Caleb held a pair of tongs in his hand. He passed them to his sister. "Just turned the potatoes and corn." He gave Jon a cautious nod. "Mr. Garrison."

He was impressed to see Caleb speaking to his sister without being forced. "Caleb." And that he was participating in a normal activity like grilling…well, it reeked of growth.

Caleb turned to Sadie. "I'm gonna go to my room now."

"I'll call you when supper's ready." Sadie smiled as her

brother went back into the house. She turned the wattage on Jon when the door clicked shut. "We're making progress."

"I see that. Well done." He had to look away—the brightness of her smile reached her eyes and made his stomach clench. "Is there something I can do?"

"Why don't you pour yourself some tea. The glasses are in the cabinet over the microwave."

"Would you like some, as well?"

"Oh, no thanks. I just refilled." She flashed him another smile, again making him squirm.

He headed into the kitchen, found the glasses, poured the tea, then returned to the porch, taking in the vast backyard. Several flower beds decorated the space, as well as a rock garden around the large live oak tree in the center of the yard. "You have a really great space here."

"*Merci.* It's the main reason I bought this house." She let out a soft sigh. "One of these days I'm going to build a gazebo and put a little waterfall in the rock garden."

"Lovely." His gaze steadied on her face. *She* was lovely.

Pink crept into her cheeks. "I think the potatoes and corn are ready. How do you like your steak?"

She'd made it through supper and cleaned up without making a fool of herself.

Sadie carried her glass of tea to the patio, Jon following. Caleb had excused himself to his room. "I think it's nicer out here, don't you?"

"It cools off after the sun goes down, that's for sure."

"Right. You're from up north, yes?" She lit the citronella candles on the table. Had to, or the mosquitoes would swarm.

"Nebraska."

"If it's too warm for you out here we can talk in the living room."

"No. I'm fine." He sat in one of the wooden garden chairs.

She settled in the slingback opposite him and passed him a folder. "Inside are the names of people I consider suspects in the sabotages. They fall into two categories—the workers who were laid off and the local fishermen and hunters. Both classes were vocal about not wanting the self-monitoring facilities put into the bayou areas. Well, the fishermen and hunters didn't want anything put in the bayou, man-monitored or self-monitoring. The P.I.s Vermilion Oil hired already ruled out several names."

He flipped through pages. "There are still a lot of names in here."

"Maybe you'll recognize a name or two and get a solid lead. Did you get to talk to the sheriff today?"

"I did. He's of the opinion that the FBI agents are veering down the wrong path, just as we suspected."

"They're focusing on Bruce?"

"Yes. They went by and questioned his wife's ex, trying to get him to say that Bruce had threatened him."

"Oh, no."

Jon shook his head. "The sad part is, after the guy had been badgered for almost an hour, he finally said that right after Bruce and Allie got married, Bruce had made an implied threat to the guy to stay away from Allie."

And the good news just kept coming. "Oh, no."

"I don't know if that's true or not, I'll have to ask Bruce. But long story short, Sheriff Theriot thinks they're going to continue to work that angle."

"That's so wrong." Sadie shot to her feet, injustice rendering her unable to sit still. She paced the patio, staring out into the darkness. "I can't believe it."

He moved behind her so quietly that she didn't know he was there until he touched her shoulder. She spun and faced him. With the moon shining overhead and the candlelight glimmering, Jon's golden eyes washed warmth.

Her heart pounded, thudding hard against her ribs.

"Sadie." Her name rolled off his tongue, making the butterflies in her stomach turn cartwheels. Just one word. Her name. Her legs felt as if she'd run a mile in the swamp.

While his one hand rested on her shoulder, his other came up to cup her face. He ran a smooth thumb over the edge of her mouth.

An emotion so strong it nearly knocked her over held her breath captive. She swayed.

Jon moved his hand from her shoulder, down her arm, to rest at her waist.

Her pulse raced. Her blood pressure had to be off the charts. And suddenly the air felt hot and still.

Very hot.

His eyes locked on hers. She dared not look away, not when every fiber of her being wanted to be in his arms.

Jon licked his lips and her heart flipped. Ever so slowly, he dipped his head.

"Hey, Sadie…where do you hide the spare toilet paper?" Caleb asked from the kitchen door.

ELEVEN

The sun couldn't break through the morning clouds. Saturday dawned with a promise of rain to Louisiana. Any rainfall would clear the air from the pollen coating everything in Lagniappe.

Sadie trudged down the hall to the kitchen, desperate for a cup of coffee to wake her. Sleep had teased her all night, fragments of dreams of Jon Garrison's eyes, and her brother's bad timing. Well, maybe not so bad after all—he'd killed the moment before things got out of hand. What had she been thinking? She had no idea the state of Jon's salvation, yet she'd almost fallen right back into her old habits. She groaned as she filled the coffee filter, poured water into the pot's basin and pressed the button to start the brewing.

She glanced at the clock—already after ten. Sadie was normally an early riser, but today, with little to no sleep, she dragged her heels. She glanced at the clock again. If she was up, Caleb should be, too.

Her first knock on his door went unanswered. She knocked harder the second time and called out his name.

No response.

Her heart flipped. Had the blackmailers found out she'd increased her investigation efforts? She twisted the knob and pushed open the door.

Nothing but a rumpled bed met her gaze.

Panic seized her heart in a tight fist. Had they come and taken Caleb? Carried him out to the bayou?

Sadie rushed down the hall to her room. Bile stung the back of her throat. She grabbed a pair of jeans and slipped them on, tugged on a shirt and grabbed a pair of socks on her way out. She half walked, half hopped down the hall while putting on her socks. Should she call the police? Would they believe her? Knowing what she now knew, would they even help her because she hadn't reported the letters?

Tears burned her eyes as she made her way to the kitchen door, where she kept her tennis shoes. She jammed her feet inside and turned for her purse.

"Where are you going?"

Caleb stood in the doorway, rubbing his eyes.

"Oh, Caleb. I thought they'd taken you." She rushed to him and engulfed him in a hug.

"Taken me? Who? Wh— Oh, the blackmailers." He returned the hug, if only halfway. "No, I'm fine."

She took a step back and looked into her brother's face. "Where were you? I checked your room and you weren't there."

"I was in the bathroom."

"Oh." Had she been fully awake and thinking clearly, she'd have thought of that.

The coffeemaker gave a final sigh and bubble.

"Didn't mean to scare ya." Caleb crossed to the icebox and pulled out the gallon of milk. He twisted off the cap and took a big swig.

Sadie was so relieved he was okay that she didn't even admonish him for not using a glass. Instead, she grabbed a mug and poured herself coffee. She didn't even bother to sit at the table to sip, digging her hip into the counter.

Caleb recapped the jug and returned the milk to the icebox. "Hey, Sadie, about last night…"

The warmth moving across the back of her neck had nothing to do with the hot coffee. "Yeah?"

Her brother stared at the floor, scuffing the tile with his sock. "I didn't mean to interrupt anything."

She felt like a teenager caught out necking after curfew. "You didn't."

Caleb lifted his gaze to hers. The look he tossed her clearly screamed *yeah, right.*

Well, he didn't. But two seconds later...

"I don't mean to cramp your style."

"Oh, you don't. I—I..." She clamped her mouth shut. How could she tell him she'd changed? That she'd once been that woman who had a style to cramp, but wasn't anymore?

"Hey, it's cool. If you hook up with somebody, I'm okay with that."

No. No. "No. That's not it. I'm not like that."

He met her stare.

"Not anymore."

Caleb didn't say a word, just crossed his arms over his chest and waited. Exactly who was the adult here?

She really didn't want to have this conversation. Not now. And not with her little brother. But she had no other choice. *Lord, please help me do this right.* "Before I was saved, I wasn't exactly, uh, a woman of high moral fiber." That was putting it loosely.

"Hey, none of my business."

"No, you need to know I'm not like that anymore. You might hear rumors about me around town. More than likely, they're true. Or they were." Her throat threatened to close. She forced down a sip of hot coffee. "But I'm not that person anymore." She shrugged. "I just wanted you to know."

"TMI, sis."

Huh? "TMI?"

Caleb laughed and gave her a one-arm hug. "Too much information."

She chuckled and snuggled against her brother.

Thank You, Jesus, for opening his heart.

The phone's shrill ring made them both jump. She was still laughing as she answered. "Hello."

"Good morning. It's Jon."

As if she didn't know his voice. "Good morning to you, too."

"You sound chipper. Did you rest well?"

The rascal, he probably knew she'd been up all night, thinking of him. "Just laughing with Caleb."

"Good. I have to say I'm really impressed with the progress he's making."

She smiled at her brother's retreating back. "I am, too."

"Well, glad I didn't wake you."

"Is something wrong?"

"Not at all. I have a meeting set up with Jack Kinnard."

Her heartbeat bumped up a notch as she focused on the name. "One of the disgruntled employees."

"Right. Just so happens, he's been off probation for only six months. So I have a legitimate reason to contact him."

"What was he in for?" This could be a huge break.

"Nothing as blatant as sabotage, but it's a past, which is nothing more than what the FBI has on Bruce. And he has more motive—being laid off tends to upset people."

"When are you talking to him?"

"In about twenty minutes."

While she wanted to hear what he said, she knew she couldn't go with him. But she couldn't just sit around and bite her nails. "Should we meet for lunch?"

He chuckled. "I was hoping you'd say that. How about the café at noon?"

"I'll see you there. Bye." She hung up the phone and reached for her mug. She'd better get it in high gear if she was to get her shower and be ready on time.

She passed Caleb in the hall.

"Hey, do you mind if I hang out with a friend today?"

Sadie paused. "One of those guys from summer school? Sure, I don't have a problem with it. What time will you be home?"

"Dunno. Not long. He'll be here to pick me up in about ten minutes."

"Okay. I've got to get ready for my lunch date, anyway."

"With Mr. Garrison?" Caleb's voice had a sing-song tone.

"Yes. But it's about our investigation." Yet the pit of her stomach tightened.

"Sure." He chuckled as he headed to his room.

She shook her head and moved to take her shower.

An hour and a hot shower later found Sadie much more her normal self. The steam had cleared her head of the cobwebs. She had to admit to herself that she was excited about seeing Jon again and it wasn't all because of what he'd share.

Oh, Lord, I'm really attracted to him, but I don't even know if he's a Christian. He's so nice and cares about others— please let him be a Christian. I don't want to go back to my old lifestyle, but I want romance and love. Was that wrong to want love so badly it made her teeth hurt? Was it wrong to pray for that?

Sadie contacted the P.I.s, filling them in on Jack Kinnard. In turn, they removed four more names off the suspect list. She could feel them getting closer to the truth. If she could just buy a little more time with the blackmailers…

She dressed, putting extra care into her makeup application and adding a spray of perfume. The smell of flowers always made her feel confident. She grabbed her purse and shut the door, locking it behind her.

The mailman met her on the steps. "Hello there, Sadie."

"Hi, Mr. Wilson. How're you today?"

"Good. You look nice." He handed her two envelopes.

"Merci."

"Have a good day." The elderly man crossed the front yard toward the next house.

"You, too," she called out as she glanced at the mail.

She froze as she registered the return address on one of the envelopes. Department of Corrections. Sadie rushed to the car and got behind the wheel. She turned over the engine to get the air-conditioning humming before she slit open the envelope.

A cover letter explained that the probation officer's initial interview and house visit reports on Caleb were enclosed.

Jon.

Sadie smiled and moved to the reports. Her heart skipped a beat.

It is of this probation officer's professional opinion that the minor shows no current ability at rehabilitation.

Oh, really? She'd just see about that probation officer's *professional opinion.*

He couldn't wait to see Sadie.

Jon sat in a back booth in the café, eyes glued to the front door, nerves in a tight wad. He couldn't even sip the ice water the waitress had left for him.

He'd thought about Sadie last night after he went home. A lot. And he'd come to the conclusion that he wanted to get to know her better. Not for his job.

As a man romances a woman.

Oh, he wanted to tell Sadie that Jack Kinnard was definitely a prime suspect, that much was true, but he wanted to just see her even more. Just stare into her eyes. And maybe, if he was lucky, get the kiss her brother had thwarted last night.

His meeting with Jack couldn't have gone better as far as extracting information went. Jack was belligerent and openly hostile against Vermilion Oil. When Jon had asked what Jack thought about the sabotages, he'd replied with, "They get what they deserve." Very much worth a second look, which is exactly what Jon intended to share with Sheriff Theriot.

After he told Sadie.

Something about Kinnard's attitude seemed almost gloating in nature. The way he smirked.

Jon glanced at his watch—she was already eight minutes late. Where was she?

He'd tossed and turned all night. Recalling how soft Sadie's face had been. Remembering how slight her waist felt in his hand. Anticipating what it'd be like to kiss her. It'd been a long time since he'd felt like this over a woman and the exhilaration fed his adrenaline.

And then she was there, breezing through the door. She glanced around the tables.

He stood and waved, not bothering to hide his wide smile. His heart did silly things whenever she was near.

She made eye contact with him and headed in his direction. He continued to stand beside the booth, determined to be the gentleman and treat her like she deserved—like a lady. As she drew closer, he noticed the firm set of her mouth, the narrowness of her eyes. What had stolen her good mood from earlier?

Had there been another sabotage? He was working as fast as he could in trying to help the sheriff in the investigation.

She stopped less than two feet in front of him. Her eyes glimmered…with anger. At him.

All the air left his lungs. "What's wrong?"

"What's wrong? What's wrong?" Her voice had a shrillness to it he hadn't heard before.

"Sit down and you can tell me what's happened." He motioned to the booth.

"I'm not sitting down with you, you rat. You snake." She grew louder.

The waitress paused, holding an empty tray. People near them stared. He kept his voice low. "What'd I do?"

"What did you do?" She shook her head. "How can you ask that?"

"Sadie, please. I don't know what's made you so mad."

She popped her fists onto her hips. "*No ability for rehabilitation? Are you serious?*" Her voice raised at least two decibels.

Oh, no. His report. She'd gotten her copy. "I can explain. That was before I—"

"What, stabbed me in the back? Let me think you cared about me, when you were only trying to get the dirt on my brother?"

He reached for her. "No, it's not like that. Just si—"

"Don't touch me and don't tell me what to do." She was flat-out yelling now and didn't seem to mind. "I can't believe I thought you were different. I thought you were special. You aren't. You're just like all the other user guys I know. At least with them, I knew what I was getting into bed with."

She grabbed his glass of water from the table and tossed it in his face. "You're worse than they are—you're a fake. I'm sorry I ever met you."

Sadie turned on her heel and stormed from the café.

He pulled several paper napkins from the dispenser and dabbed at his face, still staring after her, even though she was well out of sight.

"Looks like you blew it, buddy," a fellow diner said.

The guy was right. He'd blown it good this time.

And hadn't a clue how to fix it.

TWELVE

Cooyon! She'd acted just like a *coyoon*. Sadie slammed the side of her fist against the steering wheel. How could she have made such a scene in public? She'd lost control of her tongue. And her actions, apparently. She'd actually thrown water in Jon's face. Was she resorting to her old ways? Mortification settled in her chest. *Dear Lord, please, no.*

It mattered not that part of her anger had been righteous—defending Caleb when he'd begun making great strides in rebuilding his life. There was never an excuse for moving out of the will of Father. She'd given in to her anger just as she had in the past. She was supposed to be beyond this. Tears fell as she jerked the car to the side of the road. It shuddered to a stop in a cloud of dust.

Condemnation oozed over her like water from a soaked sponge. No, Pastor had told her that was wrong...that was the great liar whispering to her. The Holy Spirit moved in her—conviction, never condemnation. And her spirit knew what she had to do.

She lowered her head until her forehead rested against the steering wheel. From the depths of her heart spoke her soul. *Father, forgive me.*

While a blast of emotion didn't wash over her immediately, she knew she'd been forgiven. She dried her tears, checked the rearview mirror and steered the car back onto pavement.

She'd just pulled into the driveway, killed the engine, stepped up to the porch and unlocked the front door when a car whipped in behind hers. The engine hummed as Caleb exited from the passenger seat. Sadie stared for a moment, realizing she recognized the car from somewhere. But where? When Caleb shut the door and gave a wave, the car backed out of the driveway and turned. She caught a glimpse of the driver—Lance Wynn.

"Hey. You're home early from your lunch date." Caleb lumbered up the stairs to join her on the porch.

"I didn't know you knew Lance. I thought you said you were going somewhere with your friends from summer school."

"No, you just assumed that. I just said I was going out with a friend." He pushed open the door and stepped into the foyer.

Sadie followed, welcome coolness surrounding her as she shut and locked the door behind her. "But Lance? How do you know him?"

Caleb headed to the kitchen and retrieved a soft drink. He popped the top and took a long swig before narrowing his eyes and studying her. "You look like you've been crying. What's wrong? What happened?"

She'd have to show him the copy of Jon's report. Would it make him revert to his sullenness? Make him feel like if he was going to be perceived in a certain manner, why should he be different? She knew that mentality well—had lived it for many years.

He set the can on the counter and let his arms dangle. "Sadie, what happened?"

She blinked away the tears. "I, uh, had a disagreement with Jon."

"About your friend?"

"Not exactly." She leaned against the bar stool and picked at the loose paint.

Caleb straightened and crossed his arms over his chest. "About me?"

She sighed. No point in delaying putting the ugly truth out in the open. She reached into her purse and pulled out the papers and passed them to her brother.

He frowned, scowled and then his face turned as red as the

soda can on the counter. "No ability for rehabilitation?" His stare met hers.

She swallowed past the lump lodged in her throat. "I know. I'm so sorry, Caleb."

"And he sent a copy of this to the state?"

"Yes."

He tossed the papers onto the counter. "What'd he say when you confronted him?"

"Well, he didn't say much. But to be fair, he didn't have much opportunity."

Caleb huffed. "Don't see why you should be fair. He wasn't."

"I shouldn't have acted as I did, though. That was wrong of me."

"What'd you do?" Her brother's eyes lit up.

She ducked her head. "I threw a glass of water in his face."

Caleb's laughter brought her head up with a snap. His deep laughter, a sound she'd never heard, warmed her. And it was contagious. She giggled. Snorted. Then flat-out laughed. Hard. Until tears seeped from the corners of her eyes.

She covered her mouth and fought to stop chuckling. "I shouldn't have done that. It was wrong."

"It's funny." Caleb kept laughing.

"It is now, but it wasn't then. And it was in the café, at lunchtime on a Saturday, so it was pretty full."

Caleb chuckled harder. "Bet he was embarrassed."

That sobered her. "And I should apologize."

"After what he wrote? Not hardly."

Oh, part of her so agreed with her brother. But her spirit determined otherwise. "You've heard the saying that two wrongs don't make a right, yes?"

"Yeah. So?"

Oh, Father, help me with the words that will reach him. Open his heart to Your understanding and wisdom.

"Well, he was wrong in what he reported, no argument there, but my being ugly doesn't change his report, does it?"

"Doesn't change it, but sure makes ya feel better, don't it?"

She considered her emotions, not willing to lie to Caleb. "At that moment when I threw the water in his face, yes, I felt like I had *done* something about an injustice."

"See?" He smiled wide.

"But that's wrong, Caleb. It doesn't change anything in his report, now does it? All it did was embarrass him and make me feel bad for acting out. It accomplished nothing."

"But it made you feel better when you actually did it, right?"

"And that's my point—we can't act on feelings. Or we shouldn't."

"Who says?"

Sadie took a deep breath. "Scripture."

"So you really do read the Bible and believe all that?"

"With all my heart and soul, yes."

"Hmm." He wore a pensive expression. "So, about the report. What do we do?"

He'd had enough of the spiritual talk for now. That was okay—she remembered how she'd had to have lots of little doses before she was ready to hear the big parts. Had to plant the seeds before they could be nurtured and grow. "Now that I've calmed down, I realize that was his initial report. From the first day in his office and his first home visit. Things have changed since then."

"You mean I'm not rude and obnoxious anymore?" Laughter crept into his voice and eyes.

"Well, I wouldn't go that far...." She giggled. "But, I think his next report will be more favorable. As long as he doesn't mention my behavior today." She shrugged. "I guess I should've let him explain. That's probably what he tried to say."

Caleb stared at her in a serious, contemplative way. "You like him, don't you?"

"I do like him. What he's doing for our friend goes well beyond his job. That says a lot about a person, yes?"

"No. I mean you like him, like him. Like flowers-and-candy-type like him."

That lump had returned to her throat. "You mean romantically?"

"Yeah. You like him in that romantic-y way, right?"

And she'd just determined she wouldn't lie to Caleb. She let out a heavy sigh. "Yeah, I think I might."

"The report aside, he hurt your feelings because he didn't tell you about it."

The kid was too astute for his age. "*Oui.* But I guess he had his reasons."

"What's God say about hurting someone else's feelings?"

She was really out of her element. She'd been a Christian for only a year, not someone who'd been studying God's word for years and could spout off Scripture at the drop of a hat. But Caleb waited for an answer.

God, I need a little more help here. Give me the words to bring glory to You.

"Well, you should never do something to intentionally hurt someone else."

"That's in the Bible?"

"Not exactly like that, but basically, yes."

"No matter if they're good or bad?"

This witnessing business was so much harder than she'd ever thought. It'd looked so easy for Pastor and his wife when they'd led her to Christ. "I don't think we get to play favorites. God doesn't." A flash quickened against her mind again. "Scripture says, 'Be devoted to one another in brotherly love. Honor one another above yourselves.'" *Wow, thanks, God. You're so good.* "I think that's pretty clear that we don't get to pick and choose who we honor and who we don't."

Caleb nodded. "Yeah, I guess I get that." He shoved off from the counter. "But I still don't have to like what he put in his report. Or that he hurt your feelings."

And that last sentence brought new tears—ones of joy—to her eyes.

Self-disgust didn't come close to how he felt.

Jon drove around Lagniappe, not even paying attention to his direction. All he knew was that he'd insulted and hurt Sadie at a critical time in their blooming relationship. A relationship he'd been more excited about than he'd ever thought possible.

He could kick himself. He needed to apologize and explain. More apologizing than explaining.

It suddenly dawned on him that he'd headed toward Sadie's house without conscious intent. His subconscious knew where he needed to go. Had to go.

One right turn later and his car crawled down her street. All of a sudden, his mouth went dry and adrenaline pushed through his veins. He eased into her driveway, both relieved and anxious to see her car parked under the carport. Apprehension slowed his movements as he tromped to the porch.

What was he going to say to her? Would she even agree to see him? He wouldn't blame her if she didn't.

The front door swung open before he'd even made it to the steps. Caleb's hulking form centered on the porch after closing the door behind him. Afternoon shadows caught the stubble on the young man's set chin.

Great. He'd have to explain his report to Caleb, as well. There was no doubt in Jon's mind that as upset as Sadie was, she'd shared the report with her brother. He took a tentative step toward the porch and nodded. "Caleb."

Caleb moved to block Jon's ascension. "Mr. Garrison." Oh, yes, by his tone and demeanor, Caleb definitely knew about the report.

"Is your sister here?"

"Yep." Caleb crossed his arms over his chest. He wouldn't make this easy.

Jon jammed his hands into his pockets. "Can I see her?"

"I don't know, can you?"

"Cute. Please tell her I'm here." Unease made Jon pull his hands from his pockets to hang limply at his sides.

"You know, you really hurt her. Hurt her feelings. Made her feel like garbage." Caleb glared. "You made her cry. That's not cool, dude. Regardless of what you think of me, that was low. She didn't deserve that."

She'd cried? Jon wanted to sink into a hole and let the grass cover him. "I need to explain to her. To you, too."

"Hey, dude, what you put in the report is your business. I know how you guys are—thinking you're above the rest of us because of the power you hold over us. Hold it all in your hands. God-complex and all that. I don't care about your power or your stupid opinion."

"You don't?" Jon hadn't been prepared for that. Well, he hadn't been expecting the God-complex analogy, but he could understand how Caleb would perceive a probation officer as such. He'd been prepared for Caleb to argue his ability to rehabilitate. To disagree with the entire report.

"Nah, dude. Your opinion matters to the state, sure, but to me? I couldn't care less what you think of me."

That statement was more like the Caleb he knew. Jon could handle a belligerent kid. "So why are we standing out here having this discussion?"

"Because what I do care about is that you hurt my sister. She does care what you think. And she wasn't hurt so much by what you wrote but that you didn't tell her. She just got that in the mail and it blindsided her." Caleb shook his head and continued to glare. "Not cool at all, dude."

As if Jon didn't feel like a heel enough.

"Especially considering you were makin' your move on her last night."

The back of Jon's neck felt as if it were being jabbed by a hot poker. "It wasn't like that." What did the kid know?

"Yeah, whatever. Tell me you weren't going in to suck face when I busted out on the patio last night."

Maybe the kid *did* know something after all. "I really don't think it's appropriate to discuss this with you."

Caleb took the steps two at a time, stopping mere inches from Jon. "I think it's very appropriate. She's my sister, my only family. She's a good person, not somebody you toy around with."

Jon noticed the moisture in Caleb's eyes, mixing with fierce determination as the young man continued. "I haven't been around many honest-to-goodness good people in my life, but she's one of them. I won't let you hurt her."

"I didn't mean to."

"Maybe not. But right now, she's resting. I think you should leave."

"But I need to apologize to her. Explain."

Caleb raised a single eyebrow. "Why don't you give her some time? I don't think she's up to seeing you just yet."

Which meant she was still mad, understandably so. Jon considered the protectiveness in Caleb's eyes—almost reflective of the look in Sadie's eyes when she'd tossed the water in his face.

"Okay. I'll go. But I intend to call her later."

Caleb shrugged and took a step backward. "Your funeral, dude."

Jon got back into his car and drove toward his house, replaying his conversation with Caleb over in his mind. He was struck by two things: he'd hurt Sadie to the point where she'd cried—talk about really blowing it—and Caleb had changed faster than anyone Jon had ever seen in his career.

Which made him question if he'd become too cynical to do his job.

In the past week, he'd learned he was wrong about Sadie, and now about Caleb. He was batting zero in the judgment department.

THIRTEEN

"Father, Son and Spirit, Give me grace, that I, Still may live a Christian, And a Christian die." The last organ note of the song held as if being lifted on seraphs' wings.

Sadie closed the hymn book, her heart full of God's glory. Beside her, Caleb stood still, quiet and respectful. He looked handsome in his khaki slacks and polo-style shirt. She'd been worried he'd fight about attending church with her, but he hadn't. Hope filled her that Caleb, with his questions and perception, would soon hear the call of Christ.

Pastor Bertrand lifted his arms. "Please, bow your heads."

As one, the congregation bent their heads.

"Heavenly Father, we thank You for Your love and mercy, and for Your Son, Jesus Christ. Through His blood, all of us are washed clean. We pray You will walk with us as we leave from this place and go out into the world to shine Your light. In Jesus's precious name we pray, Amen."

Sadie always felt filled with the Spirit of God after every service of Pastor's. Today was no different. She cut another glance at Caleb. Had he been moved?

They filed into the aisle toward the door.

The former voodoo priestesses Tanty Shaw and Marie LeBlanc, now new but very strong Christians, stopped to meet Caleb. "We're so glad you came today, Caleb. It's nice to have you here."

Caleb lowered his head and responded in muffled tones. Sadie understood well how it felt to be addressed by older ladies. Most teens just felt uncomfortable. She put her hand under his elbow. "I want to speak to Pastor. It was lovely seeing you ladies." She kept leading him down the aisle, weaving around other members of the congregation filing out from the pews.

When they reached Pastor, Sadie gripped his hand. "Wonderful message today."

"*Merci.* Felicia's waiting outside for you." He released her hand and took hold of her brother's. "And you must be Caleb. Nice to have you worshipping with us today."

Caleb mumbled a reply, then stuck to Sadie's heels as she made her way down the stairs toward the parking lot.

Felicia Trahan-Bertrand stood chatting with her cousin Monique Harris and Monique's fiancé, Deputy Gary Anderson. Felicia smiled widely as Sadie and Caleb approached. "Good morning, Sadie. I wanted to ask you and your brother to our house for lunch. We always have a few members over. Say y'all will come, yes?"

Who could resist the woman with such grace and gentleness? Sadie glanced at Caleb, who'd taken a sudden interest in the cars parked in the lot. No help. She turned back to Felicia. "We'd love to, *merci.* What can I bring?"

"Nothing. I put on a big pot of gumbo this morning."

Sadie's mouth watered at the mention. Aside from being a lovely person, Felicia was one of the best cooks in the parish.

"Y'all just head on over to our place. We'll see you there straightaway." Felicia linked arms with Monique and moved toward her car.

Sadie touched Caleb's arm. "Come on."

Once inside the car, she broke the silence. "If you don't want to go to Pastor's for lunch, I can call and give our regrets."

"Nah, that's fine."

"You don't mind?"

"For gumbo?" He laughed, breaking the awkward tension.

She joined in. "And Felicia's one mean cook."

The drive was short, but peaceful. Caleb stared intently out the window. Sadie's thoughts went to Jon.

She needed to apologize to him for her behavior. It was inexcusable. She'd acted out of anger and hurt—emotions that shouldn't dictate her actions. As soon as she saw or spoke to him, she'd ask his forgiveness.

Something had occurred to her during Pastor's sermon this morning. She'd been more hurt by Jon because she'd begun to open her heart to him. That'd never happened before. Oh, she'd been involved with men before, many men, but she'd always known she wasn't the marry-and-live-happily-ever-after type of woman in their mind.

But Jon was different. With him, she wasn't constantly reminded of her shameful past, because he never treated her that way. He opened doors for her, bought her meals out, wasn't afraid to be seen in public with her. Maybe it was best that he wasn't local, so he didn't care as much what others thought.

"Can God forgive anything?" Caleb's voice jerked her from her woolgathering.

"Well, now, there is one sin that is considered the unpardonable sin."

"So what's this unpardonable sin?"

"You know, Pastor can answer your question much better than I can."

Her brother turned red. "Nah, that's okay. I don't want to know that badly."

She parked the car and laid her hand on his wrist. "Caleb, never be embarrassed to ask questions about God and salvation. I'm just saying I'm still learning and growing in Christ, so I have a hard time explaining." She patted his arm. "Pastor's a good man, but he has a not-so-flattering past. He knows how it feels to be treated like a second-class citizen. He'll answer your question and won't make you feel stupid, if that's what you're worried about."

Relief marched across Caleb's face. She caught movement from her peripheral vision. "Look, Pastor's outside by himself. Would you like to ask him while there's no one around?"

Caleb ducked his head and looked at her through his lashes. "Will you ask him for me?"

"Sure. Come on." She opened the door and stepped onto the driveway. "Hey, Pastor."

He turned and approached. "Hello. So glad y'all could make it."

Caleb stood silently beside her. *Lord, this could be what he's been searching for. Please surround him with peace and open his heart to Your word.* "Pastor, I was wondering if you could explain the unpardonable sin to my brother. I'm having a hard time on my own."

Pastor Bertrand tilted his head and looked at Caleb. "Of course."

Caleb's brows bunched. "What's that mean?"

"Basically, denying Jesus is God's son, profaning the Spirit of God is the unpardonable sin."

"So everything else is forgiven?"

"If you've accepted Jesus as your Lord and Savior and you confess, ask for forgiveness and repent in your heart, then yes."

"Even if you broke the law?"

Pastor laughed and tossed his arm over Caleb's shoulder. "Son, come with me. I have a story to share with you."

Caleb moved easily with Pastor Bertrand. Sadie felt like an intruder on a spiritual bonding moment. *Thank You, Father, for putting the questions on his heart at the right time, when Pastor was able to answer and share. I beg You to touch his spirit, Father.* With tears in her eyes, she climbed the steps and knocked on the front door of the house.

CoCo opened the door. Sadie took a step back. She knew CoCo was married to Felicia's brother Luc, but she hadn't expected CoCo to be here.

The woman didn't look stunned to see Sadie. CoCo stepped onto the porch and motioned Sadie toward the porch. She hesitantly joined the alligator conservationist on the swing.

CoCo rested her hands atop her protruding tummy. "I didn't intend to ambush you. I just wanted to talk with you."

Sadie didn't trust herself to speak, but didn't want to come across as a mute *cooyon.* "About what?"

"Whatever you did to get Mr. Wynn to shut down those facilities in the bayou, well, it's very much appreciated."

Sadie's heartbeat slowed back to normal. "Well, he's very interested in protecting th—"

"Oh, puhleeze." CoCo laughed. "I know good and well Deacon Wynn is most interested in protecting his pocketbook. So I know the suggestion came from you and I just wanted to thank you."

"You're welcome."

CoCo looked out to the bayou. "I know you think I don't like you because of Luc."

Sadie's heartbeat returned to racing speed.

"But that's not true." CoCo stared into Sadie's eyes. "I used to be jealous of you because men were drawn to you, but I never disliked you."

Swallowing hard, Sadie struggled to find her voice.

"What I'm trying to say is, can we be friends? I respect how you've changed your life and would really like to get to know you better. And I know how hard it is. I think some people will always remember me as a voodoo priestess."

Sadie chuckled. "And I've hoped people would forget about my past."

"Accept it…we might forever be known as the voodoo priestess and the harlot." CoCo laughed louder and looped her arm through Sadie's. "But we'll face 'em all together. Look at how far we've come." CoCo patted her belly. "Who would've ever thought I'd be the maternal type?"

They stood and walked to the front door. Pastor and Caleb approached, both wearing smiles. CoCo dropped her arm and stopped Sadie. "Oh, I did want to warn you about something."

"What?"

"After I heard you'd gotten Wynn to shut down the wells in the bayou, I called the group and told them. Nearly everyone seemed satisfied."

Pastor and Caleb reached the porch steps.

"Thanks. I appreciate your doing that."

"Well, there's one man who isn't happy. A Derrick Roberts." CoCo lowered her voice. "He's a hunter and he's a little unstable. We've locked horns before because he sometimes poaches gators out of season."

Sadie's pulse thrummed. "What do you mean by unstable?"

"I think he could get violent if he doesn't get his way. I'm just warning you to watch out." She smiled brightly at Caleb. "Hey, *Boo,* I don't think we've been introduced. I'm CoCo."

Derrick Roberts could be violent and he was unhappy with her? Could he be unhappy enough to try to blackmail her?

Her driveway sat empty.

Jon parked on the curb in front of Sadie's house. He'd tried to call her last night, but there'd been no answer. Not even voice mail. Who in this day and age didn't have an answering system of some sort?

After a sleepless night, he knew he couldn't go another day without apologizing and trying to make things right between them. So here he sat, in front of her house, waiting for her to return. She was probably at church, he surmised.

Church. Religion. Salvation. They were all fairly foreign ideas to him.

Oh, up until his parents had died as a teen, he'd been raised to believe in God and His Son, Jesus. But then he'd gone to live with his aunt Torey, who'd told him God was nothing more than a glorified Santa Claus. After the way she'd treated him, he'd begun to believe her. What kind of God would take his parents and leave him in the care of his irresponsible aunt? But lately, he'd begun to understand that he should have continued in his parents' faith and ignored his aunt's nonsense.

Now he wondered why he'd ever given her the power over his faith.

He realized Sadie was genuine. Her faith was real, life-changing. Hadn't her faith been what prompted her to turn her life around and become the lady she was today? *That's* the kind of faith he wanted. The kind of faith his soul yearned for. So, at five-something this morning, he'd done something he hadn't done in years—pulled out his Bible and read. He ended in *Romans* 12. Tears leaked from his eyes as he finished reading verse eight. Jon set the Bible on the table and fell on his face, praying to God and asking forgiveness for being so angry, and so weak.

Tires sung on pavement beside him, drawing him from his musings.

Sadie emerged from her car, staring back at him. Now or never. *God, please help me apologize right.* He slowly made his way up the driveway. "Sadie, please hear me out."

"I'm so sorry for my behavior, Jon. Please forgive me."

Whoa! Not at all what he expected. "No, I understand. Let me explain."

She raised a single palm in the air. "No explanation necessary."

Befuddled, he glanced at Caleb leaning against the trunk of the car. Not a shred of belligerence or ill-will lingered on the boy. He turned his attention back to Sadie. *Thank You, God.* "Then let's both forgive each other and move on, shall we?"

Sadie smiled and his world righted. "Agreed. Come on in. I have something interesting to share with you." As she headed up the walkway, she told him about the potential suspect—a possibly violent and very unhappy Derrick Roberts. Jon made a mental note to check the name tomorrow.

The three of them were on the porch before he noticed Sadie and Caleb had both gone stiff and tense. He followed their stares. A white envelope lay on the mat in front of the door. An envelope with Sadie's name written in black, in bold letters.

He reached for it just as both Sadie and Caleb spoke.

"No."

"Don't touch that."

He grabbed the envelope and darted his stare between Sadie and her brother. "What's going on?"

Sadie blinked rapidly, then looked to Caleb. "We might as well tell him, yes?"

Caleb shrugged. "Whatever you think is best."

Curiouser and curiouser, as Alice would say. "What?"

"Come inside." Sadie hurriedly unlocked the door and rushed inside, glancing over his shoulder. "How long were you parked in front of the house?"

"Maybe ten minutes. Why?"

"Did you see anybody around the house?" Caleb asked.

"No."

Sadie slammed the door shut and dropped her purse on the buffet.

"Would someone please tell me what's going on?"

She waved to the living room set. "Sit down." She took the envelope from his hand as she followed him.

He planted himself on the couch, while Caleb chose the chair and Sadie perched on the arm. "Please tell me what's wrong."

"Just a second." She ripped open the envelope and pulled out a piece of paper. Caleb leaned forward to read over her shoulder. She gasped.

He couldn't take it anymore. He grabbed the paper from her hands and read.

LAST WARNING. IF YOU DON'T BACK OFF OF YOUR INVESTIGATION, YOUR BROTHER IS GATOR FOOD.

Blackmail?

"This is because you're helping me about Bruce?" He ached to think he'd brought this on her.

"No. It started before you approached me, when I began my investigation into the sabotages at Vermilion Oil."

And then it dawned on him. They'd both recognized the envelope. They'd recognized it because this wasn't the first one.

"Let me see." How had she been dealing with this alone?

She moved to her purse, pulled out two envelopes and tossed them in his lap before returning to the arm of the chair.

He read the first two letters, his gut tightening. "Why didn't you tell me?"

Tears shimmered in her wide eyes. "Because I was afraid if you knew, you'd think I couldn't protect Caleb and would take him away."

Caleb leaned forward and patted his sister's back.

"Have you taken these to the police?"

"How can I?"

"How can you not?" She couldn't deal with a blackmailer on her own.

"You yourself said that truth and justice are less important than convictions."

He hadn't put it as eloquently, but that was the gist. "But this is different."

"No, it isn't. The first thing law enforcement would do would be to remove Caleb from the house, yes?"

"I honestly don't know." He'd never had a situation similar to this come up, not in all his years of being a probation officer.

"We weren't willing to take that chance. I stay here." Caleb's voice was firm.

"But you have to tell someone."

"The letters say not to." Sadie squared her shoulders. "And I'm not going to give them a reason to come after my brother."

"But what if they come anyway? You haven't stopped investigating, and you couldn't protect him if they did come."

"Dude, I can protect myself."

They were both crazy.

Jon shot to his feet. "You can't be serious."

Sadie rose, as well. "I'm dead serious. And you can't tell the police, either."

"Oh, yes I can. And I need to."

She grabbed his arm. "You can't. It's not your place to tell."

"Come on, Sadie. This is serious. A man's been murdered and the murderers are threatening you."

"I'm taking it seriously, but I can't let you go to the police. They explicitly said not to. And because they're murderers, I need to play by their rules. I've made it a point to not publicly work on the investigation, but we're making progress."

Which explained her terms about working with him to help Bruce. Now it all made sense.

"But, Sadie…"

"Please. Just let me do this my way."

Her eyes pleaded with him. His heart felt like it was caught in a vise. Against his better judgment, he nodded. "But I'm kept aware of any letters from them. Anything at all out of the ordinary, you let me know immediately."

"Agreed." She smiled.

He prayed he wasn't making the biggest mistake of his life.

FOURTEEN

What in tarnation was going on?

Sadie parked her car and scrambled to her office building early Monday morning. Members of the press hung around the front door like ants at a picnic.

"Ms. Thompson, what's the status of this latest facility?"

Oh, no. Not again. Why hadn't Deacon called her?

She shoved past the crowding mass. "No comment at this time."

"What do you mean *no comment?* You're the PR rep." Jackson Devereaux stood face-to-face with her.

"It means I'm gathering details. I wouldn't want to report anything not factual, now would I?" The sarcasm rolled so easily off her tongue.

A security guard opened the door and grabbed Sadie inside. She let out a heavy breath. *"Merci."*

"Looked like they were about to devour you."

"I'll say." Sadie glanced at the faces milling about, staring out the window at the blood-sucking press. "Where's Mr. Wynn?"

"Haven't seen him since he came in and headed to his office." Hiding?

She winked a thanks to the guard and hustled to the elevators. How could Deacon let her get blindsided? Had he just given up? Gone down without a fight? That wasn't Deacon Wynn. Especially when they were getting so close to a solution. She'd spent the better part of last night talking with the P.I.s and narrowing down the names of suspects.

The elevator door slid open and Sadie marched down the hall to his office. Irritation caused her to forget manners or diplomacy. She opened the door without bothering to knock, tossing her purse and briefcase onto the credenza.

Deacon and Lance stood toe-to-toe, faces red and veins in their necks and foreheads bulging. She'd have to deal with the issue of the latest facility in a moment. "What's going on in here?"

Her boss glared. "I thought I told you to keep a leash on him."

"I'm not a dog to be leashed, I'm a man." Lance's fists hung off tensed arms.

"Then why don't you act like one?" Deacon looked as if he'd have a heart attack any second.

"Whoa. Back up a second, guys. Lance, sit over here. Deacon, take your seat."

Surprisingly, both did as she directed. She pinched the bridge of her nose. Why did every Monday have to be a beast? "Okay, let's get me up to speed, yes? Deacon, what's got you so hot under the collar?"

"Why'd you have him give a statement to the press?"

"I did—"

"I told you, she didn't know anything about it. I made the decision on my own." Lance clenched and unclenched his fists.

Deacon wagged a finger. "You didn't have the right. You've made a bad situation even worse."

"Hang on." She turned to Lance. "What, exactly, did you tell them?"

"Just that the Wynn family wouldn't rest until we got to the bottom of the situation."

She turned back to Deacon. "I don't see anything wrong with that."

"That's not all he said."

Feeling as if she were caught in a tennis match gone bad, she faced Lance. "What else did you say?"

"They asked me about my involvement." He shrugged. "I just told them that I was working with my father to see justice served."

"Go on, tell her what else you said."

Sadie tossed Deacon a stern look, then focused on Lance again.

"Well, they asked if the rumors about Vermilion Oil going bankrupt were true."

Her heart pounded. "What'd you say, Lance?"

"I was trying to make light of the situation."

"You were not," bellowed Deacon.

"Shh." Sadie held her hand up to her boss, but continued to stare at Lance. "What'd you say?"

"That we'd only go bankrupt if Dad's wife got her hands on his checkbook."

Deacon scowled. Sadie bit back a groan. Of all the childish things...

"Okay. This is ridiculous. I'm sick of this petty stuff." She shook her head. "Lance, I think you'd better leave."

"I was only trying to be funny. I want to help."

Deacon shot to his feet. "You've helped enough as it is. Get off my property or I'll call security."

"Lance, just leave." She so wasn't in the mood for a family crisis. Not when she had to find out about the facility.

He stormed from the office, slamming the door behind him. The pictures on the wall shook.

"Look, Deacon, we don't have time for this right now. Fill me in on the latest facility. How badly is it damaged?"

"Pretty bad. It had forty wells connected to it."

"Tank valve tampering again?"

Her boss shook his head. "No, this time, it was shot."

"What?"

"I think because we'd vamped up security. Somebody shot it from far enough away to not be caught by the worker on duty."

"What does law enforcement say?"

"Well, the FBI won't touch it because nothing was leaked."

"Surely the sheriff's taken an interest?" Sadie sat on the edge of the chair Lance had vacated.

"He retrieved the bullet and is running tests. That's all I know."

"Why didn't you call me?"

"Lance told me you'd given a statement."

"I didn't."

"But you'd told him what to say last time, so I just assumed you'd been in contact with him this morning."

Sure, it kinda made sense, but still...

"When I heard him say that about Candy-Jo, well, I just blew up. I ordered him to my office." He shook his head. "I swear, that boy's turned out to be a bad apple. Spoiled rotten and jealous of anyone who might get a piece of what he thought was his. But I showed him."

"Okay, I don't need to know all this." She stood and smoothed her skirt. "I'm going to call the sheriff and see if he's got anything yet, then I'll figure out something to tell the press." She retrieved her belongings and moved to the door. "And next time, call me."

Sadie rushed to her office, set down her purse and briefcase and sank into her chair. She rubbed her temples as Georgia set a steaming cup of coffee before her.

"Why didn't you call me in early?"

"I just found out when I got here."

"Oh. Lance said you'd given him a statement."

"That's a lie."

"Oh, my." Georgia's brows shot up. "No wonder Deacon hauled him up to the office."

"Yeah, it wasn't pretty."

Georgia clapped her hands. "What can I do to help?"

"Try to get Sheriff Theriot on the phone. See if he knows anything about the bullet used yet."

Georgia nodded and rushed out. Sadie pinched the bridge of her nose.

Father, what am I missing?

The sooner the case was solved, the sooner the blackmailers would leave her alone. Then she could continue on with a normal life. With her brother. And Jon.

She shook her head, clearing her thoughts. She had to focus. Turning on her computer, she opened a blank document and began work on the press release she'd give out. Not that she'd talk to those vultures downstairs. No, she'd just pass out the release and be done with them.

Georgia stuck her head in the doorway. "Sheriff Theriot's not available to give us any information. Wanna try someone else?"

Who else could she ask? Wait a minute! "See if Deputy Gary Anderson's available. Wasn't he recently named Chief Deputy?"

"Right. I'm on it." Georgia's head disappeared.

Sadie finished her statement, did a final read, then printed it out. The printer had just spat out the last copy when Georgia hollered, "Deputy Anderson on line two for you."

She took a deep breath, punched the number and lifted the receiver. "Hi, Deputy Anderson. It was so nice to see you at church on Sunday."

"Likewise. What can I do for you?"

"As you know, I'm with Vermilion Oil. I know the sheriff's been working on tests on the bullet retrieved from our damaged facility. Mr. Wynn's terribly concerned. I'm just checking to see if y'all have any information yet." She held her breath and waited.

A sigh came over the phone, followed by—was that a groan? "We just got a positive ballistics match."

Adrenaline made her heart race. "And?"

"The bullet that was found in the facility is a perfect match to the bullet used to murder Harold Daniels."

Urgent, that's what Sadie had said.

Her phone call had been ambiguous at best, cryptic at worst.

Just that she had some new information and needed him to meet her for an early lunch at the café.

He sat in a front booth, watching and waiting for her. What had happened? She wouldn't tell him—said she couldn't discuss it over the phone. If the blackmailers had threatened her again, he'd...

He'd what? As he analyzed his emotions, he realized he'd been about to think that he'd kill them. No, he wouldn't go there. He and God had just gotten back on speaking terms and Jon was pretty certain God wouldn't approve of murder threats.

The bell tinkled over the front door. Jon caught sight of Sadie making her way to him. Her face was flushed and her blond hair was wind-mussed.

The waitress had been about to set down his glass of water, but halted as she spied Sadie, as well. "Think I'll just hold on to this for a minute."

He wanted to smile, but Sadie reached them right then. She glanced at the waitress, took in the glass, and her face flushed even more. She smiled shyly at the other woman. "I owe you an apology."

The waitress set the tray on the table, as if she'd drop it if she didn't. "Excuse me?"

"I'm sorry for the way I behaved the other day. That was terribly rude of me and I made a mess that someone else had to clean up. I'm very sorry."

The waitress stared at her with a dumbfounded expression. "Uh, okay." She set the glass on the table and lifted the tray. "Can I get you something to drink?"

"Iced tea, please." Sadie slipped into the booth seat opposite Jon.

What a woman. Jon reached across the table and took her hand. "That was really nice."

"I owed her the apology."

"Well, what's so urgent?"

Her words tumbled out over one another. About a facility being damaged, this time by gunshot. The bullet matching that of what killed the man in the picture—the man the blackmailers had murdered.

The waitress appeared with Sadie's tea. "What can I get y'all?"

"The lunch salad special, please," Sadie replied without even looking up.

"Make it two."

The waitress whisked away.

"Sadie, this means the murder, the blackmail and the sabotages are all related."

"Right. I mean, I knew the sabotages were involved, otherwise, why would they demand I cease my investigation? But this just doesn't stop." She smiled and shook her head. "Guess I'm not as bright as I thought."

The thought of her in danger had him tightening his grip. "You *have* to go to the sheriff now."

She jerked her hand free and frowned. "Nothing's changed in regards to how I feel about following the blackmailer's instructions, Jon."

"Then why the urgent call?"

"Don't you see? Because now the FBI will have to stop looking at Bruce."

Jon racked his brain to figure out what she meant. "I'm sorry, but I'm not following you."

"He's on probation, right? That means he can't have a gun."

"Oh, Sadie, I wish it were that simple."

"Now I'm not following."

The waitress returned with Cajun chicken salads. She set them on the scratched table and left.

Jon took Sadie's hand again. "I'll bless the food." He bowed his head and offered up a short prayer of grace. When he was done, he raised his gaze to meet Sadie's.

Tears danced in her eyes.

"What?"

"Nothing." She cleared her throat and reached for the pepper. "So what's the problem?"

"If the FBI thinks Bruce is guilty, they'll just assume he got an illegal gun to use."

"Oh." Her face fell. "Then we need to ramp up our investigation."

FIFTEEN

The rain came down in sheets, washing Lagniappe clean.

Sadie ran a mental list of things she had to accomplish this Tuesday as she drove in to work. The long-awaited rain splattered against the windshield. She could only pray all the evidence had been gathered from the latest facility sabotage.

Hiding under the shelter of her umbrella, Sadie rushed into Vermilion Oil.

"Nasty out there, isn't it?" The receptionist handed Sadie a stack of paper towels.

"*Merci.* It's coming down in different directions." She blotted her skirt and blouse, not sure how much protection the umbrella had provided. She tossed the napkins in the trash, closed her umbrella and left it in the stand, then smiled quickly at the receptionist as she made her way to the elevators.

Georgia met her in the hallway. "Only a few die-hard media cats showed up this morning. I told them we had no new information since your statement of yesterday. I think standing out in the rain discouraged them from hanging around."

Sadie chuckled and put her purse and briefcase on her desk. "Yeah, it's torrential out there." She took a napkin and swiped the raindrops on her purse. "I heard the sheriff's pulled all his deputies to work the case now. Maybe they'll get a decent lead."

"Oh, an Ethan Hebert phoned you about ten minutes ago. He needed information about his pension benefits."

"I can't help him. Direct him to Human Resources."

"I already tried that. He said he needed to talk to you." Georgia set a cup of coffee on Sadie's desk. "Said he also needed to talk to you about the sabotages."

Sadie froze and stared at her assistant. "What'd you tell him?"

"I told him I'd take his name and number and have you return his call, which he refused, saying he'd call you back later, then I called the sheriff."

"What'd the sheriff say?"

"That they'd check it out, see where the call originated from. Did you know the office phones are tapped?" Georgia shook her head. "Have been since the FBI got involved in the case."

"I didn't know, but it doesn't surprise me."

"Hopefully the sheriff will get some answers and let us know something."

"I hope so." Sadie pinched the bridge of her nose. "Come find me when I'm not at my desk if he calls again, though. Maybe he does have something important to say."

Georgia nodded. "You got it. I'm going to go over the numbers of producing wells, just in case you need the figures for another press release."

"*Merci.*" Sadie watched her assistant leave, the enormity of her job weighing down her limbs. She hadn't heard from Deacon yet this morning. Or Lance. Was it too much to hope that the two had worked out their differences? Probably.

The phone rang. "Sadie Thompson."

"Ms. Thompson, this is Ethan Hebert."

"Yes, my assistant told me you'd called. I'm sorry, but I have no control over the pension benefits."

"So I heard."

"She told me you'd mentioned something about the sabotages against our facilities." It was a statement, but she'd deliberately made it come out as a question.

"I don't know if you know Jack Kinnard or not."

She tingled all over. "I know the name."

"Couple of months ago, he was talking to some of us who were laid off. All mad. Said we had to send a message to the company. Said any of us that were serious about making our point to Mr. Wynn should come by his place later."

Every muscle in Sadie's body tensed. "Did you? Go by his place?"

"Yeah. I wanted to hear what he was thinkin' 'bout."

"And?"

"He was talkin' crazy. That we should mess up the wells to make Mr. Wynn realize he needed us."

Sadie gripped the phone tighter. "Was anything planned?"

"I don't know. I thought he was just talkin', but I didn't want to be no part of it, so I left. I never heard anything else."

"Did you tell anyone about this?"

"Nah, didn't seem like anything more than talk, until I heard about the facilities."

"Why haven't you called before?"

"Been working offshore for the last three weeks. Just got back in town last night and caught up on the news."

"Thanks for letting me know, Mr. Hebert." She hung up the phone and lifted it right up again. She tried to intercom Deacon, but got the busy signal. Excited, she switched over to the phone again and punched in the number for Jon's cell phone. After three rings, the call was dropped in voice mail. She left a hasty message, then disconnected.

Her intercom buzzed. Probably Deacon now. She lifted the receiver. "Sadie Thompson."

"You have a delivery down here." The receptionist's voice carried a teasing-type tone.

She didn't have time for the media's tricks. "What kind of delivery?"

"The kind every woman loves to get."

Flowers? Candy? "I'll be right down." She made her way down the hall and into the elevator. Who would send her something?

Jon.

Her smile widened as she crossed the floor to the reception-ist's station. A large bouquet of fresh flowers sat atop the counter. "Oh, my…are these for me?"

The receptionist matched her grin. "That's what the envelope says. Are you holding out on us about a secret romance?"

Warmth spread through her stomach up into her chest. "No. This is a surprise." She grabbed the vase. "I'm going to take these to my office."

"What? And not let me know who your admirer is?"

Sadie was saved from having to answer by the phone ringing. She quickly headed back to the elevator. Leaning in, she inhaled deeply. They were beautiful flowers and such a big arrange-ment! Her heart stuttered. They had to be from Jon. How sweet and thoughtful.

Back in her office, she set the vase on the work table adjacent to her desk. Her entire office would smell like a field of wild-flowers. She loved it.

With trembling fingers, she gently removed the envelope from the plastic holder. She turned it to read the outside. Her stomach tightened as her heart raced. No florist name. Only her name.

In black block letters.

She collapsed into her chair and sank back into the smooth kid leather, gripping the envelope. No, it couldn't be. The florist had to have just used a blank envelope by mistake.

Only one way to find out.

She opened the envelope and pulled out the card.

WE WARNED YOU.

The card fell to the desktop. Her heart beat loudly. Her entire body shook.

In one fluid movement, she shoved the vase of flowers into the trash can and reached for her purse.

Georgia rushed into the office. "What's wr—" She spied the flowers in the trash and stared at Sadie. "What's happened?"

Sadie snatched the card and envelope and shoved them into her purse. "I have to go. I have to leave now. Let Deacon know and handle anything that comes up." She moved around the desk toward the door.

"Is there anything I can do to help?"

"No." No one could help her. Except...

Jon.

She flipped open her cell as she stepped into the elevator and dialed his number.

"Hello."

Just hearing his voice made her break. Tears ran freely down her face. "Jon. They sent me flowers."

"Sadie? Who sent you flowers?"

"*They* did. At work. Said they'd warned me."

"Where are you now?"

"On my way to the school."

"No, let me check there since the school will be letting out soon. You go home and wait for him."

"Okay. But what if they've g—"

"Don't think like that. Just go home and wait for Caleb. I'll be there soon."

She shut the phone and stepped off the elevator. After drying her eyes, she stopped at the receptionist's station. "Did you happen to recognize the florist logo on the van that delivered those flowers?"

"Ah, someone wants to remain anonymous, huh?" The receptionist shook her head. "Sorry, I was on the phone when he walked in with them."

"What about when he left?"

"I was calling you and admiring the flowers. Besides, it's raining so hard out there who could see?"

"Thanks." Ignoring her umbrella in the stand, Sadie rushed to her car. She nearly slipped on the slick pavement in her haste. Jerking open the door, she tossed her heels onto the passenger-side floorboard and slid behind the steering wheel. Water rivulets dripped from her hair into her lap. She closed her eyes, tears falling again.

Lord, please let Caleb be okay. Keep him safe. ·

Blackmailers sending flowers?

The danger slammed against Jon as he sped along the wet roads to the school hosting the summer program. He gripped the steering wheel tightly, leaning forward. The air from the defroster flared against his face. He blinked several times, focusing on the road ahead. What a time for the rain to decide to come. Weeks of sweltering heat with only hints of rain and today, of all days, it decided to downpour.

What seemed like an eternity later, he turned into the circle in front of the school, behind the buses. Jon ducked against the pounding rain as he ran into the office.

The lady at the desk glanced up. "My, someone forgot their umbrella, didn't they?"

He didn't have time for niceties. He flashed his probation officer's badge. "I need to know if Caleb Frost was in attendance today."

"Certainly." The woman pushed glasses on her nose and clicked on the computer keyboard in front of her. "Yes, sir. He was here today."

"What bus number does he ride?"

She typed more. "Number eighty-three."

"Thank you." He turned and ran back to the circle. Two buses were already on the main road. The last two were inching up the circle. Jon ran to catch them. He moved beside the last bus, squinting to catch the number.

Twenty-four.

He sprinted forward, ignoring the rain as he gained on the first bus. Pumping his legs faster, he moved alongside it as it slowed for the turn.

Number sixty-four.

He'd missed it. Jon turned and ran back to his car and seeped inside. He was drenched through and through, but it mattered not. He cranked the engine and pressed hard on the accelerator. Tires spun on the wet pavement, the end of the car fishtailing. Jon straightened the nose and eased off the accelerator. The car moved to the road.

Caleb had to be on his bus, heading toward Sadie's. He'd arrive safe and sound and Jon would find both brother and sister at the house. The blackmailers were just messing with her.

Please, God, let it just be that.

He reached Sadie's street and caught sight of the flashing red lights on bus number eighty-three in front of Sadie's house. Two boys got off. Neither one was Caleb. The lights went off on the bus and the vehicle lumbered down the road. The two boys moved toward the opposite end of the street, slowly enough that it was evident they didn't mind the rain.

Jon pulled up alongside them and rolled down the window. Didn't matter that rain poured in—he'd already soaked the velour seats. "Hey, isn't Caleb Frost normally on that bus with you?"

"Yeah." One of the boys hitched his backpack higher on his back.

"But he wasn't on it today?"

"Who are you?" the other boy asked.

Jon fished out his badge and flashed it. "Now, was he on the bus today?"

"Was this morning, not this afternoon."

Gut clenching, Jon nodded. "Thanks." He rolled up the window and whipped into Sadie's driveway.

She stood on the porch, looking like a drowned rat. "He wasn't on the bus, was he?" Her voice quivered.

He ran to the porch and took her in his arms. "No, but he was at school today, all day. So they didn't have him when they sent you the flowers."

"But they knew school would be getting out soon and they'd grab him." Tears mixed with the rain on her face. "They had it all planned."

"But we know they haven't had him long." He kissed the

crown of her head. "Sadie, we have to call the sheriff. Time is of the essence."

She stiffened in his arms for a moment, then went slack. "Okay." The dejection in her voice ripped the heart from his chest.

He led her into the house. She went to grab some towels while he made the call to the sheriff. She returned as soon as he hung up the phone.

She passed him a terry cloth towel. "What'd he say?"

"I explained, and he's a little ticked you didn't report the blackmail letters, but he knows the primary focus now has to be on finding Caleb. He and those FBI agents are on their way here now."

"Do the agents have to come?"

"Technically, yes. It's a kidnapping of a minor and that falls under federal jurisdiction." He rubbed his head with the towel.

"Great."

He tossed the towel onto the back of the bar stool and reached for her. She was warm against his chest. "We'll find him."

Her body shook as she sobbed. "It's all my fault. They warned me, but I didn't listen."

"Shh. It's not your fault. It's going to be all right."

"I didn't back off the investigation. I put my brother, whom I was supposed to protect, directly in harm's way."

"No, you didn't. These guys were targeting Vermilion Oil before Caleb even got to Lagniappe. They're the criminals and the ones to blame, not you."

Her cries intensified and he held her tighter.

Lord, please let it be all right.

SIXTEEN

Sadie twisted her hands in her lap, staring at Sheriff Theriot and the two FBI agents. "And that's all I know."

"He was at school today, but never got on the bus," Jon interjected.

"You should've called us as soon as you got the first letter," Agent Ward said with a sneer. "We could have prevented this from happening."

Oh, why not just hand her the ticket for a guilt trip?

Jon's grip on her shoulder tightened, providing her with the strength she needed. She relaxed under his touch.

"Well, I didn't. So we need to get moving now. We know Caleb's been missing less than an hour. We need to be out in the bayou looking for him."

"We know how to do our jobs." Agent Lockwood was just as arrogant as his counterpart. "We'll take it from here."

Sheriff Theriot stood and put his cap back on. "My men know this area better. I'll order my deputies to start making tracks around the bayou. We'll call in the dogs, see if they can get Caleb's scent now that the rain's slacked off."

"In case we weren't clear, Sheriff, this is our case and we'll run it as we see fit." Ward stood and nodded at Lockwood. "We'll have a team over here from New Orleans in less than two hours."

"Two hours! Caleb could be dead by then. If he isn't already."

Sadie swallowed back the tears. She wouldn't give these *cooyons* the satisfaction of seeing her cry. But they needed to get off their duffs and find her brother.

"Ma'am, we know what we're doing. You stay here and call us immediately if you hear anything." Agent Ward passed her a business card. "Wait for our men to get here. We'll set up a phone tap, have agents on-site in the event we're needed."

"Bu—"

"We'll report in when we know something." Agent Lockwood led the way to the front door.

The two agents left without another word.

Sadie felt as if her world was coming to an end. In a sense, it was. Why hadn't she listened to Jon and turned the letters over to the sheriff before something happened to her brother?

"Listen, I'm going to follow up with this Ethan Hebert. I'll keep in touch." Sheriff Theriot tipped his hat and left.

"I can't just sit here and do nothing." Sadie stood and paced. Where was Caleb? Was he okay? Was he scared?

What if Caleb was alive, waiting for someone to rescue him? Those FBI agents didn't know the area…didn't know the bayou at all. Even the agents from New Orleans would be no help.

"Why don't I call Spencer Bertrand to come over and sit with us?"

"Okay." Maybe Pastor would be able to share with her some Scripture to comfort her. A promise from God that everything was going to be all right.

Father, please protect Caleb. He's my brother, but Your son.

While Jon moved to make the call, Sadie ran over ideas in her head. If Derrick Roberts was the one who had Caleb, he knew the bayous inside and out. The FBI didn't stand a chance of finding Caleb in time.

Spence is on his way. He's bringing Felicia.

Kind, sweet Felicia, who cooked like nobody's business. Had it only been two days since they'd broken bread together?

Wait a minute…there was someone who knew the bayous

better than Derrick or any other hunter. CoCo! She knew every tree, limb and alligator.

Could she ask CoCo to search the bayou in her condition? Then again, the woman had continued making her bayou runs. If she was unable to get out in the bayou in this heat, maybe she'd know someone who would help.

Finally feeling as if she were doing something productive, Sadie passed a shell-shocked–looking Jon and grabbed the phone. Then she realized she didn't know CoCo's phone number. She yanked the phone book off the buffet and flipped to the right section, praying CoCo and Luc had a listed number.

Thank You, Jesus. She found the number and pressed buttons. Luc answered on the second ring. "Hello."

"Luc, it's Sadie. I need to talk to CoCo. It's urgent."

"Sure. Hang on." A clunk sounded over the line, followed by Luc yelling for his wife, then muffled voices.

Seconds fell off the clock, feeling like hours before movement sounded on the connection. "Hello."

"CoCo, it's Sadie. I need your help."

"What's up?"

Sadie took a deep breath and filled CoCo in on the blackmail letters, Caleb being missing, the FBI's ineptitude and her belief that her brother was already in the bayou somewhere. She struggled to keep the emotion out of her voice so CoCo could understand her.

"I'm on it, *Boo.* Here, jot down my cell phone so you can keep me updated." CoCo rattled off seven numbers.

"*Merci,* CoCo, but are you sure you're up to going out and searching in this heat? In your condition?"

CoCo laughed. "Girl, I'm pregnant, not an invalid. Besides, Luc won't let me go alone anymore, so he'll be with me."

"I really appreciate this."

"I'll call if I find anything."

The line went dead. Sadie hung up the phone and turned to Jon. "Smart thinking."

Now that she'd made the call, she felt helpless again. Nothing to do but sit around and wait. This was her brother in danger!

Jon collected her into his arms, holding her close enough that she could hear the beating of his heart. It calmed her. His lips connected with her temple. She closed her eyes and leaned into him, drawing strength and resolve from him.

With his knuckle under her chin, he lifted her face and stared deeply into her eyes. Sadie's heart beat double-time. Her mouth went dry.

Ever so softly, barely more than a feather's graze, his lips moved against hers. She felt dizzy but alive. She reached for him with both hands, running her fingers through the back of his short hair.

He dipped his head again, kissing her gently.

Bam! Bam! Bam!

Sadie jumped out of Jon's embrace. For a moment, disorientation ruled her mind. Disorientation and peace. And then she remembered why Jon was here. Caleb was missing!

Bam! Bam! "Sadie? Jon? You in there? It's Spence and Felicia."

Sadie rushed to the door and flung it open. Felicia wrapped her arms around Sadie's shoulders. "I'm so sorry for what's happened. Come on, let's go to the kitchen and get some hot tea brewing."

Before Sadie could gather her thoughts, Felicia had her in the kitchen, pulling out the kettle.

Pastor's and Jon's voices rumbled from the living room.

"Now, that's on, yes?" Felicia flipped the stove on high. "So, fill me in. What's happening?"

As Sadie went through the tale again, Pastor walked in and stood behind his wife. When she was finished, she felt spent. Wasted. Drained.

"We've been praying, of course. What else can we do for you?" Pastor's face was wreathed in concern.

"Nothing. The FBI are doing whatever it is that they do. The sheriff's following up on a lead I got this morning. CoCo and Luc are out in the bayou, looking around." Sadie shook her head.

Lord, please let Caleb be okay.

"CoCo knows the bayou area best out of anyone in the whole state." Felicia's eyes were still blinking with tears. Pastor put his arm around her waist.

Sadie glanced into the living room, saw no one, then looked at Pastor. "Um, where's Jon?"

"He said he was following up on a lead, for me to stay here with you and he'd call us if he learned anything."

Why hadn't he told her himself? She wasn't some weak little woman unable to handle stress. "Did he say what lead?"

Pastor shrugged. "Didn't say. Just told me it'd take only half an hour or so. I wouldn't worry about him if I were you."

Like she didn't have enough to worry about at the moment.

Felicia moved and put her arm around Sadie. "Honey, you look pretty worn-out. It could be a long afternoon and night. Why don't you try to get some rest?"

Rest? As if. "I don't think I could."

"Then why don't you take a hot shower? It'll refresh you, invigorate you. Maybe you'll remember something you've forgotten. Something that could help find your brother." As always, Felicia was gentle and understanding.

Sadie *was* exhausted. Maybe a shower would pep her up a little, clear her mind. "Okay. I think I will."

"I'll have your tea ready when you come out." Felicia patted her shoulder before releasing her.

Sadie trudged to the bathroom and turned on the hot water. She sat on the edge of the tub, letting the tears overtake her. Panic and fear already had a strong grip on her heart.

Father God, please keep Caleb safe until we find him.

He'd never felt so useless before in all his life.

Jon couldn't take it any longer—he'd had to leave. Had to do something. For Caleb. And Sadie.

Jack Kinnard had been off probation only six months. And Jon hadn't been so sure that the man should've been released from prison, much less gotten off with no supervised release. Yet that's what the judge had deemed to be within sentencing guidelines, so that's what he'd gotten. Maybe it was past time for a little follow-up from an officer of the court.

Jon eased his car down the street Kinnard lived on. The torrential rains had ceased to a mere drizzle. Steam drifted up from the road. Humidity hung heavy in the air.

He parked three houses down, then crept toward Kinnard's home. The lawn was desperate for mowing, a fresh coat of paint was sorely needed and the truck in the driveway needed some body work. How could the man live in such disarray?

Crouching low, Jon crept alongside the house. He felt like a DEA agent or something, going in for a bust. But he wouldn't play hero. He just wanted to nose around and see if he saw something. If he did, he'd let the sheriff know immediately. But if he saw Caleb...

A dog barked from the backyard of the house next door.

Kinnard flung open the back door. "Shut up, mutt."

Jon froze, pressing his back against the house.

"Sorry, stupid dog was barkin'." Kinnard spoke aloud, but Jon couldn't make out another person on the deck in back. He tipped his head forward and spied the man, a phone clutched to his ear. "Okay, so you got the kid. Just keep him there till I get there."

Jon's heart raced. Got the kid? Was he referring to Caleb?

"Stop whinin' and just keep him there. Feed him another line or something."

He had to be referring to Caleb, and by the way he was talking, Caleb was fine. Jon sent up a quick prayer of thanks, then tuned his ears as Kinnard spoke again.

"Look, I don't care how you keep him there, just do it. I'll head that way in a few minutes. You checked him for a cell phone, didn't you? I don't want him callin' his sister and spoilin' everything. All we've worked for."

No doubt that this man's partner had Caleb.

"Yeah, well, I'm just hangin' around here watchin' the news— see if his sister calls the police."

Despite the sticky heat, Jon went cold.

"You don't need to worry about that. I'll make that decision when I get there, see if he's worth anything."

Jon dared not move, but his mind rallied and screamed.

"Don't you start wimpin' out on me, kid. You were in on this from the beginning. Heck, boy, it was mainly your idea to bring the kid and blackmail into it."

Kid? Boy? How old was Kinnard's partner? Then again, Jon had noticed that a lot of people around town referred to others as *boy, son* and *kid.* Must be a Southern thing.

"Well, I didn't mean to hit the guy. I was tryin' to hit the facility and it was dark. Besides, his death worked out okay for us, didn't it?"

Excitement lit in Jon. He'd just overheard a confession. As soon as Kinnard got off the phone and went back inside, Jon could get out of the man's yard. He couldn't wait to call the sheriff and tell him what he'd overheard. Probably a really good idea to not be caught here.

The dog growled at the fence. Only four feet away, Jon held his breath. If Kinnard moved two steps toward the fence, he'd see Jon.

"I told you to shut up, ya stupid mutt." A scraping sounded, then a crushed-up beer can hit the fence. The dog yelped and moved away.

"I'm gonna check the local stations one more time, then I'll head that a-way."

A door slammed.

Jon leaned forward and stuck out his head. No sign of Kinnard. Jon let out a long breath, then as quietly as he could, turned and crept back toward the street.

He reached the front porch.

Da-da-daa! Da-da-daa!

Jon reached into his pocket and pressed the button to reject the call on his cell phone, then moved his finger to the button to place the cell on silent. He stood very still, listening and waiting.

Maybe Kinnard was in the back of the house and hadn't heard. Maybe he'd had the television up loud. Maybe Jon was home-free.

And then the dog next door began barking and growling and jumping on the fence.

The front door opened.

Kinnard's stare settled on Jon's. They held eye contact for a long moment, then Kinnard flew off the porch.

Jon turned and ran all-out toward the car. Kinnard's footsteps sloshed and thudded behind him.

Two hundred feet more and he'd be there.

Each step felt like an eternity. His feet slipped on the wet grass and he went to his knees. He popped back up, got his balance and took off again.

One hundred more feet.

Still running, he hit the pavement. While running, Jon stuck his hand in his pocket and pulled out his keys.

Fifty feet more.

Jon's loafers slid on the slick asphalt. Down he went. He put his palms to the road, tried to push upright.

Excruciating pain slammed into the back of his head. He fell back to the wet pavement. White dots danced before his eyes, and just before everything went pitch-black, one thought went through Jon's mind.

Jesus, help me.

SEVENTEEN

He'd rejected her call! It'd rung once, then went directly to voice mail—a sign that the recipient had turned it off midcall.

Sadie placed the phone back in the cradle. She sat on the edge of the bed, thinking. Why on earth would Jon reject her call? They'd made a connection today that took their relationship to a new level, even if they hadn't had time to discuss their feelings. He wouldn't abandon her and then reject her call. There had to be something wrong with his cell.

Maybe the battery was dying. Or maybe he was somewhere he couldn't get a good signal. She'd just take her shower and then try him again.

She glanced at the clock as she made her way into the bathroom. Caleb had officially been missing for almost four hours now. How could this have happened? Why hadn't she gone to the police when she'd gotten the first letter? Whatever made her think she could handle it and take care of Caleb by herself?

She washed the tears away in the shower, shampooing her hair twice, just to say she did. After her shower, she brushed her teeth and slipped on walking shorts and a T-shirt, then headed into the bedroom.

Steam swept across the room, having made its great escape from the confines of the bathroom.

Felicia had been right—a hot shower had helped clear her

head. But in doing so, her heart ached harder. While under the hot jets, she'd realized just how much Caleb had come to mean to her. Not just because he was the only family she had left. Not just because he was her half brother. But because they'd begun to form a relationship like she'd dreamed of when she agreed to become his guardian. And now she stood to lose him.

Father, please bring Caleb safely home to me.

She slipped her feet into sandals and paced. She checked the caller ID base—no call registered from anyone. Not the sheriff. Not the FBI. Not Jon.

She perched on the edge of the mattress and dialed Jon's number again. It rang four times before dumping her into his voice mail. No way he'd ignore any call, much less hers. And he couldn't still be out of range. Not unless…

She retrieved the business card the FBI had given her from the pocket of the skirt she'd been wearing before her shower. With no further thought, she lifted the phone again and dialed the number.

"Agent Ward."

"This is Sadie Thompson."

"Yes? Have you heard from your brother?"

"No. Nothing yet."

"Ma'am, we're working the case. We'll call you as soon as we know something." His impatience seeped into his voice.

"Wait. That's not why I'm calling."

"Did you think of something that could help?"

"No. I'm calling about Jon Garrison."

"Who?"

"The probation officer. Caleb's probation officer."

"What about him?" The FBI agent all but sighed over the connection.

"He left my house to go follow a lead. I think something's happened to him." Raw fear twisted inside her.

"Why's that?"

"I called his cell phone and he rejected my call. I tried calling again and it eventually went to voice mail."

Now the agent did sigh. "Ma'am, I'm sure he's just fine. If you left a message, he'll probably call you back. Now, I really need to get back to working on your brother's case."

She wouldn't let him disregard Jon's predicament. She *knew* something was wrong. "No. Something's wrong. Didn't you hear me say he went out to follow a lead?"

"A lead on what?"

"My brother's case."

The agent cursed under his breath. "What lead?"

"I don't know for sure."

"Do you have any idea where he might have gone?"

"We were looking into Derrick Roberts or Jack Kinnard. He could've gone to follow up with either of them."

"Wait a minute. He's a probation officer?"

"Yes."

"What's his cell phone number?"

She gave him the number. "But he's not answering."

"I'm not going to check that. Hold on a minute."

She could make out the sound of keys on a computer keyboard clicking.

"I got it."

"What?"

"All cell phones of government officers have a GPS in them. Right now, the satellite's showing Mr. Garrison is moving."

"Moving where?"

More clicking sounded. "Um, looks like he's heading outside the city limits."

Her heart clutched. "Toward the bayou?"

"Yes, wh— Look, I'll call you back when we know something." He hung up the phone without so much as a goodbye.

At least he'd figured out this was serious.

Sadie replaced the phone, her entire body shaking.

Something had happened to Jon and now he was going toward the bayou. Had he found Caleb? The blackmailers?

The murderers?

Sweet Jesus, watch over Jon and Caleb. Please. I love them both.

And as she whispered the prayer, she knew beyond a doubt that she loved Jon Garrison with everything she had. Just when she thought she'd cried until she had nothing left inside, tears streamed down her cheeks. She dropped to her knees beside the bed and laid her face on the mattress.

Darkness enveloped him as his right thigh vibrated. Jon couldn't open his eyes for a moment.

Movement jarred him against hot metal and he jerked. His head hurt. The back of his neck hurt. Matter of fact, his whole body felt beat-up. He tried to swallow, but his mouth met with cotton.

Jon slowly blinked open his eyes. Attempting to hoist himself from his reclining position, Jon fell against the restraints holding his legs together and his hands confined. Fear surged through his soul as it all came back to him.

Jack Kinnard had him!

A quick glance around confirmed his fears. He lay tied up and gagged in the back of Kinnard's beat-up pickup truck, a tarp of some sort covering him. The truck bounced and swayed, definitely not on a paved road. The smell of diesel exhaust and damp soil crept under the covering to tickle Jon's nose.

God, I need some serious help.

What had happened? Jon pressed his eyes closed, even though he could feel his right eye swelling. He needed to clear his head, think. He remembered the phone call, running, slipping and falling, then nothing but blackness after that. Kinnard must have hit him from behind, knocking him out.

Now Kinnard was taking him somewhere. Well, Jon needed to do something. Get himself free so when the truck stopped, he could stand up to Kinnard. Or at the very least, get away from the man and his partner.

Jon scooted across the bed of the truck, pressing his back against the hump of the tire well. Anything to have some stability. The jarring metal grated against his spine, but he ignored the pain. He had much more pressing concerns.

Where could Kinnard be taking him? Remembering the phone call he'd overheard, Jon considered that he was most likely being taken to where Caleb was being held. At least he'd know if the boy was okay.

His right thigh vibrated again. Poor Sadie, she must be frantic. She had to be the one calling.

God, comfort her. Somehow, let her know I'm okay.

His phone! Kinnard hadn't thought to check Jon's pockets and remove the cell. He could call for help! If he could just get the phone out of his pocket...

But his hands were tied behind his back. He tugged and wiggled his wrists, but the makeshift cuffs didn't loosen. By the rough feel, Jon could only guess that a nylon rope held his hands in place.

The truck took a sharp right, rolling Jon to the other side of the bed. Metal clanked against metal. Jon maneuvered himself into a more comfortable position. Maybe he could use whatever was loose in the bed to get his hands free.

He shifted his bound feet, making large sweeping motions. He kept moving in a clockwise manner. His legs were tired, his back aching and his breathing coming in spurts, but he kept searching. Surely he'd hit upon something soon. As he made yet another semicircle, metal clattered.

Success!

Jon moved his legs slowly back until he felt an object under his calf. The truck hit a bump, bouncing him and the object a good three inches off the bed of the truck. He landed with a thud, the sound of metal tinkling hit somewhere behind him.

Great. He'd have to start all over. *Please, God, give me a break here.*

With a deep breath, Jon extended his body as much as he could and swept his legs across the bed of the truck. His thigh vibrated again.

His heart broke for Sadie. Oh, he wished he'd talked to her before he followed through on this harebrained idea. First Caleb went missing and now look at the situation he'd gotten himself into. If only he'd at least let her know how much she meant to him, how important and precious she was.

The truck made another sharp turn, rolling Jon across the bed again. And then it came to a shuddering stop.

Brring!

Sadie raced the last few steps to the kitchen and yanked the cordless off its base. It rattled to the counter. She pressed the talk button. "Hello."

"Sadie? It's Georgia. Are you okay?"

She sighed, disappointment covering her. "I-I'm sorry I ran out on you." Her voice cracked. How could she tell anyone what was going on?

Felicia passed her a cup of tea.

"I was worried. Is there anything I can do?"

She was terrified there was nothing anyone could do. Dare she open up and let someone know she was hurting? Time to forget worrying about what others would think of her. "You can pray. My brother's missing."

"Oh, no, I'm so sorry. Of course I'll pray for you and your brother."

Sadie blinked. She hadn't realized her assistant was a Christian. Georgia didn't attend Vermilion Parish Fellowship. "Th-Thank you."

"Do you need anything? Can I bring you over supper or something?"

"No, I couldn't even think about eating right now, but I appreciate the offer. More than you know." Sadie swallowed the lump in her throat that seemed to be making return appearances quite often these days.

"I'll be praying. You call me if you need something, girl. I mean it, I'm here if you need me."

Sadie thanked her friend and said goodbye, hung up the phone, then stared at the caller ID. Why hadn't she heard from the blackmailers, now kidnappers? Shouldn't they contact her again? Or were they merely going to follow through with their threat and kill him?

She crumbled against the Formica counter.

Pastor was there in an instant, keeping her from falling. How symbolic…just like he'd kept her from falling back into her old way of life, now he literally kept her steady as he walked her to the kitchen table.

Felicia sat beside her, rubbing her shoulder. "Shh. It's okay to be scared, terrified even. You don't have to hold it all together for us."

"Well, you might want to stiffen up because of who just pulled in the driveway." Pastor nodded toward the window.

Sadie shot to her feet. "Jon!"

"Oh, no, I'm sorry. It's the men the FBI sent."

Great. Someone else to tell her she'd messed up everything by not reporting the letter as soon as she'd gotten it.

"Here, take a sip." Felicia lifted the cup to her.

Not much for hot tea, Sadie took a short sip. A knock pounded on the door. Pastor moved in that direction. Men's hushed voices filtered into the kitchen. Maybe Pastor would make them go away. She didn't know how much longer she could keep up the charade of being calm. Not when everything within her screamed.

Pastor returned to the kitchen. "They're putting the tracer on the phone in the living room."

"Merci." She forced herself to take another sip. "What do we do now?"

Felicia smiled. "Just like you told your friend, pray."

EIGHTEEN

The tarp ripped away.

Jon squinted his eyes against the sudden light, even though dusk drew near. The tailgate dropped with a heavy thud. Kinnard leveled a gun at him. Not just any gun, but a forty-five Desert Eagle. Mighty powerful handgun. Powerful and deadly. All logic and reason fled, replaced with raw fear.

"Slide down here. Don't try nothin' funny or I'll shoot you." Tobacco spittle hung in the corner of the man's mouth.

Complying, Jon forced his sore and stiff muscles into moving as he'd been instructed. When he reached the tailgate, Kinnard grabbed him by the collar and jerked him into a sitting position.

Jon swallowed against the gag in his mouth. *Dear God, I'm not ready to die. Not here. Not now. Not like this. And not before I get to see Sadie at least one more time.*

"Get on yer feet." The barrel of the handgun wavered as Kinnard leaned to the side and spat.

Inching to the edge of the tailgate, Jon flexed his feet. He had no idea how long he'd been out, or riding for that matter, but his feet tingled. He jumped to the ground. His legs wouldn't support his weight and he fell onto his side.

Kinnard laughed and nudged him with the toe of his steel-toed boot. "Some big man you are. Can't even stand up. Ya wimp."

Jon brought his knees up to his chest and rolled until he was on his knees. Kinnard jerked him up by the scruff of his neck.

Jon swayed for a moment when Kinnard released him, then steadied. It felt like pins and needles shot through his feet, but he refused to fall again. Not before this man.

Lord, give me strength.

He glanced around, trying to get a sense of where they were. The bayou, that much was certain. Drops of water dripped from the Spanish moss draped over the cypress tress. The air smelled like rain and fish, both clean and polluted at the same time. A little wood-planked shack nestled against trees, as if tucked into a forest. He hadn't a clue where he was; he never ventured far out of town and surely not out into the bayou.

Kinnard waved the gun in front of his face again. "I'm gonna remove the rag from your mouth. You scream or start talkin' without me askin' you a question, it goes back in or I shoot ya. Got it?"

He nodded. As if he'd scream. Who'd hear him out here?

With the roughest motion possible, Kinnard ripped the rag from his mouth and tucked it into his pocket. Jon wet his lips, trying to get rid of the grease taste. By the looks of the rag, Kinnard used it to clean tools or something. That alone was enough to make him want to gag, but he was too scared Kinnard would shove it back in his mouth if he retched.

"Now ya wanna tell me why you was snoopin' 'round my place?"

Jon's mouth was still dry. He swallowed hard.

"I asked ya a question." Kinnard leaned and spat again. "I want an answer."

Oh, God, what do I say? Give me the words.

"Well, I came by to ask you a few more questions, then remembered I had an appointment."

He never saw the back of Kinnard's hand coming. It connected with the side of his head, the sheer force pushing him to the ground again. The sharp taste of metal filled his mouth. Jon rested his head in the damp ground and spat. Blood painted the grass red.

"Boy, don't ya lie to me." Kinnard grabbed Jon by the collar again and yanked him upright in one fluid motion. "Ya ran when you saw me."

Jon wobbled as he fought to keep his balance. "You started chasing me."

"Because ya ran." Kinnard pointed the gun right at Jon's head. "Now tell me why ya were nosin' 'round my place. And don't lie this time."

The front door of the little shack swung open and slammed against the wall. "What's taking you so long—" Lance Wynn froze on the top stair. "What's he doing here? He knows who I am, man."

Lance Wynn?

"Didn't have a choice. Found him nosin' 'round my yard. He ran."

"So you brought him *here?*" Lance descended the steps and ambled across the soggy ground. "This ruins everything. No way can we pay him off to keep his mouth shut like we can with Caleb."

Jon blinked, trying to think. The kid was involved with all this? Why? Why would he set out to sabotage his father's business? Especially when he was trying to get back in his father's good graces?

To get back in his father's good graces.

"Don't ya worry 'bout that. I can handle this." Kinnard spat again.

Now Jon understood. Lance started all this to get his father in a bad position. Then, he'd sweep in and *help* in the situation and the sabotages would stop. He'd be the saving grace to his father and get back in his father's will.

Lance narrowed his eyes. "Why were you poking around his house?"

"That's jest what I asked." Kinnard nudged Jon with the gun. "And we want the truth this time."

Maybe the truth wouldn't be so bad. "Well, I came because I wanted to talk to you again, follow up on our previous conversation."

Lance glanced at his partner. "You talked with him before?"

Kinnard spit. "We talked about the oil company."

"What'd you tell him?" Lance groaned.

"That's not important." Kinnard refocused on Jon. "What's important is what ya were doin' at my place."

"I wanted to talk with you some more. But before I got to the steps, I heard a dog barking out back. It sounded like it was coming from your yard, so I thought it was your dog. And then I heard voices, so I figured you were out back and wouldn't hear me if I knocked."

Kinnard nodded. "Yeah, so?"

Jon swallowed. "Well, I figured I'd just go around back and talk with you, but then my cell rang. My girlfriend called and I needed to go to her place, so I turned around and headed back to my car."

Lance glared at Kinnard again. "And because of *that,* you tied him up and brought him here? How stupid. He didn't know anything and now he does."

Kinnard waved the gun. "Then why'd ya run?"

Jon shrugged. "When you came out the front door, I realized I'd been wrong and it was probably your neighbor I heard in the back. I wanted to explain and talk to you, but you lunged off the steps and came at me. What else was I supposed to do?" He nodded at the Desert Eagle. "And looks like I was smart to run from you, don't you think?"

Please, God, let them not ask me any more questions.

"You moron." Lance punched Kinnard's shoulder. "You've made a mess of everything. First Daniels, now this."

Kinnard pivoted to face Lance. "I said I'll take care of it."

"Just like you did with Daniels? What about Caleb in there? He's not turning like I thought he would." Lance jabbed his thumb toward the shack. "Are you gonna take care of him, as well?"

Jon shifted and bent his knees a little. He swayed, but regained his balance. And realized that the rope around his wrists had loosened somewhat. Must've been the continuous falls.

"I said I'd take care of it." Kinnard spat, still holding the gun. "I've already made adjustments to the original plan."

"Like what?" Lance wore an incredulous sneer.

"Well, it was plain to me that yer daddy wasn't gonna welcome ya back. Not after you talked about his wife like that on TV."

Lance's eyes clouded. "What'd you do?"

"Don't you worry 'bout it, boy. I'm takin' care of ya." Kinnard chuckled, the rough, forced sound sending chills down Jon's back. "Makin' sure ya get what ya wanted."

"Yeah, right." Lance glanced at Jon. "Well, Mr. Garrison, I'm real sorry you got messed up in all this."

"I don't know what you're talking about."

"You know enough that you're now a liability." Lance shook his head and shot his partner a withering look. "Thanks to this *cooyon* here, you know way too much."

Goose bumps pimpled Jon's arms despite the warm breeze. *Dear God, don't let them kill me. Please.*

If she didn't hear something soon, she'd climb the walls.

While Sadie appreciated Pastor and Felicia being with her and praying with her, the idleness drove her crazy. And the FBI agent in the living room seemed to have made himself totally at home. He'd come in and took a soft drink from the icebox without asking and now sat reclined in her chair in front of the television. Nice to know her tax dollars were going to such good use.

A couple of ladies from the church had come by and dropped off casseroles and bread. Felicia and Pastor had finally given up trying to get her to eat, and sat at the kitchen table eating silently.

Sadie sat on the patio, staring at the early night's sky. The rain had cooled the air some, making being outdoors bearable. Yet she couldn't help but remember the last time she'd sat on the patio—when Jon was with her. She hurt all the more at the memory.

Dear God, please keep Jon and Caleb safe and return them to me.

She hated repeating the same prayer over and over, but that's the only thing that would rise in her mind.

The ringing of the phone had Sadie jumping out of her chair and rushing into the kitchen. She snatched the cordless, not caring if the agent in the living room was ready or not. "Hello."

"Sadie, it's Georgia. I hate to bother you, but it's an emergency."

Probably another facility down. "I can't deal with anything at work right now. I'm sorry, but I just can't."

"No, it's Deacon."

"What?"

"Candy-Jo called the board of directors, who have been calling everyone. Deacon was rushed to the emergency room a couple of hours ago."

"Oh, no. What happened?" Sadie eased onto the bar stool.

"She said they'd just finished eating supper when all of a sudden, Deacon got sick. Bad sick. He kept having spasms that wouldn't stop. She got him into the car and rushed him to the hospital."

Why did everything bad have to happen at once? "How long ago?"

"From what's been relayed down to me, about two hours ago."

Sadie glanced at the clock. Deacon to the hospital two hours ago. Jon missing for at least three hours. Caleb missing for about six. What was she supposed to do?

Father, help me. What do I do?

"Candy-Jo's beside herself. Called her sisters over from N'Awlins to come."

"Has anyone thought to call Lance?"

"After his and Deacon's latest blowup, I'm guessing not."

"It's his father, he should be notified."

"Want me to do that?"

Sadie thought for a moment, recalling that Caleb had been out with Lance. She should probably tell him that Caleb was missing. Maybe he would have an idea. "No, I'll do it."

"You need me to get you the number?"

"No, I should have it in my PDA."

Georgia sighed over the phone. "Have you heard anything about your brother yet?"

"Nothing." And each minute that flew off the clock felt like an eternity.

"I'm praying for you, girl."

"Merci."

"I'm going to head to the hospital. I'll call you when I know something."

"Thanks, Georgia."

"Call my cell if you hear anything about your brother. Bye."

Sadie hung up the phone and bent over the counter.

What was going on around here? What was she missing?

NINETEEN

"Get inside." Kinnard shoved Jon, making him fall yet again.

But this time, Jon was ready for it and wiggled his wrists. If the moron kept pushing him down, he'd be able to get his hands free.

"Stupid, he can't when you duct taped his ankles together. How's he supposed to walk?" Lance glared at Kinnard. "Cut the tape."

"I don't exactly have a pair of scissors here, boy." Kinnard spat, nearly missing Jon's head.

Lance sighed as he pulled out a pocketknife and bent. The sawing motion at his ankles allowed Jon to maneuver little inches at a time, all the while twisting his wrists. Just a little bit more…

Straightening, Lance pocketed the knife and nodded at his partner. "Help him stand up."

Kinnard grabbed Jon's upper arm and snapped him to standing. Jon wobbled a moment, the blood rushing to his feet making it painful to stand.

"Come on," Lance said.

Not one to remain silent, Kinnard waved the gun at Jon. "And don't try no funny stuff, either."

Right. With a redneck having a gun trained on him? Not hardly.

Jon's steps were slow, each one painstaking as hot stabs shot up his calves. He grit his teeth and did his best to follow Lance. If only he could get Lance alone, surely he'd be able to talk some sense into him.

They reached the stairs, Lance still leading the way. Jon

tested the rope against his wrists. Definitely more slack, but not enough to squeeze free. If he'd been knocked down one more time... And then it hit him. He didn't have to be knocked down at all.

He stepped up onto the first stair, then let himself go slack. Jon toppled off the stair to the right, landing hard against a rock and rolling. He grunted.

"Klutzy man." Kinnard sneered and chuckled.

"You don't know anything." Lance peered down at Jon. "You okay, Mr. Garrison?"

"Yeah. Just give me a minute." A really long one, too, because the rock he'd fallen on was now under him, right about where the rope around his hands was.

He shifted slightly, rubbing the rope against the rock. The binding loosened. If he could just stall for a few more moments... Jon semirolled. "Let me catch my breath for a second, okay?"

"Okay, Mr. Garrison."

Kinnard spat again. "Stop callin' him that."

Jon worked the rope against the rock.

"That's how I know him. Get over it."

"Actin' all respectful now, huh?"

The rope loosened.

"Shut up."

Kinnard waved the gun like a kid with a flag at a Fourth of July parade. "Don't talk to me like that, boy. Ya forget who yer talkin' to?"

The rock sliced against Jon's wrist, but he swallowed against the sting. The rope loosened even more.

"Just help him up." Lance sighed and crossed his arms.

Without warning, Kinnard tugged Jon to standing. "Now git up them stairs. And no funny stuff."

No kidding. Jon took the steps slowly. Did he dare fall again? He glanced over his shoulder. Kinnard held the gun trained on his head. Nope, no more falling. That was okay—

Jon rotated his wrist. He might be able to squeeze a hand free, if he worked at it. But not until Kinnard moved from behind him, of course. .

A step later and he stood beside Lance on the little landing in front of the door.

Lance pushed the screen door open and motioned for Jon to precede him into the room.

Room was too much of a word for the space. Maybe eight feet by ten, the area had a threadbare couch with springs sticking out facing a coffee table that had probably been around since the early sixties. It faced two hardback chairs. A single lightbulb hung uncased from the ceiling.

Caleb Frost sat bound in one of the chairs.

As Lance nudged Jon toward the other chair, Jon gave Caleb a look that pleaded for him not to say anything. If they found out Jon was personally involved with Sadie and Caleb, all hope for talking Lance into letting Caleb go would just fly out the window. Well, if he called the big square hole in the back wall of the room a window.

Lance lifted Jon's hands slightly to maneuver his arms over the back of the wooden chair.

Please don't let him realize the rope is loose.

When he was done, without inspecting the rope, Lance removed the rag from Caleb's mouth. "Well, looks like our parole officer has come to make a home inspection, Caleb. Isn't that nice of him?"

Caleb coughed and gasped for air. When he lifted his gaze, he wore the attitude he'd displayed the first time Jon had met him, staring at Lance with the coldest eyes Jon had ever seen on the boy. "Yeah, dude. Right. Like he's so my favorite person. Why'd you bring him out here? To torment me?"

Lance chuckled. "Yeah, I know what you mean. Always telling you to do better, to try harder…all the stupid stuff."

"You forgot him harping on every little thing, following up on you to make sure you're doing what he thinks you should be."

"Yeah."

Kinnard slammed the screen door shut. "Nice that ya boys get to play catch-up, but we got some things to decide."

Caleb turned his cold stare on Kinnard. "Yeah, dude, what's that?"

"Wasn't talkin' to ya." Kinnard spat on the dirty wooden floor and jerked his head in Lance's direction. "Me and the kid here got some stuff to talk 'bout."

Caleb's Adam's apple bobbed several times over and sweat glistened on his upper lip. "Well, don't let me keep you."

Kinnard glared. "Come on, kid." He flipped on an outdoor floodlight and stomped from the shack.

Lance shrugged and followed.

Their voices carried as they clomped down the steps and moved away into the darkness until Jon couldn't hear them. "Are you okay?" He worked against the rope as he whispered to Caleb.

"I'm fine. How'd you get caught up in this?"

"Shh. Keep your voice to a whisper." Jon strained his ears. Only the lingering notes of Kinnard's voice drifted back. "I figured out Kinnard was involved."

"I don't even know the dude, but from what Lance told me, he's a major mess-up." Caleb paused and coughed. "Lance said that his initial plan didn't involve anybody getting hurt, but Kinnard made mistakes."

Jon had figured Kinnard too dense to plan anything elaborate, that Lance had to be the brains of the unlikely duo. "I overheard Kinnard talking to Lance on the phone. He admitted he'd shot Harold Daniels. Although he said it was an accident, he was still the one who killed that man."

"Wonder whose bright idea it was to use that to blackmail my sister? Can you believe Lance actually thought I could be bought to play along with this scheme of theirs? Like I'd do that to Sadie! Who would think I'd go along with this black-mail idea?"

"Had to be Lance. I don't think Kinnard would've thought that quickly." The rope was still too tight to squeeze a hand out.

Caleb coughed again. "Then that means Lance had to be there. And they had to have a camera with them."

Jon replayed the phone conversation he'd overheard. "Not necessarily. Kinnard said he'd killed Daniels by accident when he was trying to shoot a facility and damage it. But that isn't where Daniels's body was found."

"So, you think Kinnard called Lance and had him help move the body, take the picture and send the letter to Sadie?" Caleb shook his head. "I don't think Lance has the stomach for that."

"You'd be surprised. Money can sometimes make a stomach cast-iron." If he could just get a little more slack in the rope…

"Maybe, but I just don't see it."

"Could be that Lance thought about it, brought Kinnard the camera, but Kinnard did all the dirty work."

"That sounds more likely. I still don't understand why."

"Because Lance needs to get back on his daddy's good side to get written back into the will." A little more movement made the rope loosen. Was it enough?

"Well, that makes sense now. Lance was ticked about his father writing him out because of his new stepmom."

"How do you even know Lance?"

"We were in juvie together."

Jon mentally flipped through Lance's and Caleb's files. There could be an overlap between their times of incarceration of only about two months. But behind a detention center's walls, with the close proximity, people could form fast friendships. "Look, I can almost get my hand free. If I lean up a little, walk the chair so to speak, can you get me some more room? I need only an inch at the most."

"Maybe. Let's try it. My hands are tied pretty tight."

Jon pushed his legs, taking the weight off the chair. Wouldn't do him good to make a lot of scraping noise and draw the attention of Kinnard and Lance. He wobbled, putting both feet down solid on the ground. He couldn't knock himself over. Jon not only had to look out for himself, he also had to protect Caleb.

Just as he started to take a step backward, Lance's raised voice floated in from the screen door, followed by Kinnard's yell.

They were coming back.

Jon set the chair down as quietly as he could, careful to get back in the same position he'd been in when they'd left. "Tone down that you don't like me. Might make Lance befriend you more. Maybe you can talk him into letting us go."

Their voices were about as far away as Kinnard's truck now.

"Okay," Caleb whispered back. "But one thing."

Footsteps creaked on the wooden step. Shadows fell across the screen door.

"What's that?"

"I do like you, though. Even if you are hot after my sister."

Oh, but the boy made observations at the oddest of times.

Where was Lance Wynn?

Sadie had called his cell, pretty certain that the Wynn mansion was no longer Lance's home. She'd left two messages on voice mail. Now what?

"Is there anything I can do to help?" Felicia asked.

"N—" Well, maybe Felicia and her circle of family and friends would have an idea. "I'm trying to find Lance Wynn. His father's been taken to the hospital and I'm pretty sure no one has thought to notify him."

"Lance Wynn." Felicia tapped her chin. "He's your boss's son, yes?"

"Yes."

"Let me see what I can do." She reached into her purse sitting on the counter and whipped out her phone.

"I'm going to keep trying his cell phone." Sadie moved to the patio, flipping on the outdoor lights. Something about being outdoors in the dark made her feel closer to Jon and Caleb. Why hadn't she heard anything yet?

She sank to the chair and hit the redial button. Ring one. She rested her chin in her palm. Ring two. Sadie sighed; she'd have to leave a third message. Ring three. "Hello."

Sadie sat up straight. "Lance?"

"Yes. Who's this?"

"Sadie Thompson."

"Uh. Oh."

"Listen, I hate to be the bearer of bad news, but y—"

"Look, I really can't talk right now. I'm in the middle of something."

"Lance, it's your father."

"Wh-What about my father?"

"He's sick and in the hospital."

Silence hung over the connection, but Sadie could make out ragged breathing. Just barely. "Lance?"

"What's wrong with him?"

"We don't know yet. Just that he got very ill—uncontrollable spasms—and Candy-Jo took him to the emergency room. That's all I know right now."

"Are you at the hospital?"

"No. I, well, I have a family crisis of my own happening right now."

"What's that?"

She swallowed. "My brother, Caleb, is missing."

"Missing, you say?"

"Yes." Tears threatened to explode. She stood and paced the patio, refusing to let her emotions crack again. "Anyway, Georgia went to the hospital to check on your father. It must be bad, because Candy-Jo called her sister to come from New Orleans."

"The drama queen needs attention."

"That's not nice, Lance."

"But it's true."

She'd made a mistake in calling him. "Well, I just thought you should know about your dad."

"Thanks, Ms. Thompson. I appreciate that. Nobody else

would've thought to call me." He laughed. "They didn't. No one but you has called to tell me."

"I'm sorry, Lance. I really am."

"Me, too. Hey, I hope you find your brother."

"*Merci.* Say, I know you know Caleb—do you have any idea what might've happened to him?"

"I don't know your brother, Ms. Thompson."

Sadie dropped back to the bench. "Sure you do. I saw you drop Caleb off here at the house before."

"Sorry, must've been mistaken. Look, I've got to go. Thanks for letting me know about my dad."

The connection died.

Sadie stared at the phone she held. Lance had flat-out lied. She'd seen him drop Caleb off and drive away. Caleb had confirmed it was Lance. Although now that she thought about it, Caleb had never answered her question about how the two knew each other. Odd.

Why would Lance lie about knowing Caleb?

TWENTY

Lance closed the cell phone, cursing under his breath.

Jon cut his eyes to Caleb. As soon as Lance and Kinnard had entered the room, Lance's cell had rung. He'd stared at the caller ID, frowned, then ordered Kinnard to gag Jon and Caleb. While Lance had been involved on the phone, Jon had been steadily working on the rope around his wrists.

He'd perked up when he'd realized Lance was talking to Sadie. At least she was okay. But what was she doing calling Lance?

Now, Lance paced. And cursed. He stopped in front of Caleb and took out the rag. "What'd you tell your sister about me?"

Caleb sputtered and even spat on the floor. Lance grabbed him by the chin and shook his head. "I asked you what you told your sister about me."

"Nothing, dude. I didn't say a word about you."

"She knows I dropped you off at your house. What'd you tell her about what we did?"

Oh, no. Jon wished he could tell Caleb to mislead Lance. *God, please help him.* He worked at the rope even harder, fighting not to be noticed.

"Nothing."

"Nothing?" Lance straightened, crossing his arms over his chest and looking down at Caleb. "I'm supposed to believe you didn't tell her anything?"

"She asked, but I distracted her. She was mad and upset."

Jon swallowed. Had to be the day she'd thrown water on him. The rope slipped. Almost free.

Lance snorted. "Sadie Thompson distracted? I don't think so. That woman's smart and once she gets an idea, she doesn't let it go."

Jon froze, praying Caleb wouldn't mention him in regards to Sadie.

"She'd gotten into an argument with...with a guy she was seeing."

Relief swarmed over Jon. Caleb was one smart cookie.

Kinnard chuckled. "Yeah, I've heard all about the guys Sadie sees."

It was all Jon could do not to charge into the man's beer gut. He shifted his hand. The rope moved a little more.

Lance glared over his shoulder at Kinnard. "Shut up. I'll get to you in a minute." He turned back to Caleb. "She never brought it up again? Me?"

"Never."

Lance straightened, obviously debating about whether to believe Caleb. Finally, he turned his back on Jon and Caleb and advanced on Kinnard. "Now, tell me what you did to my father."

"Huh?"

"What. Did. You. Do. To. My. Father?"

Jon worked diligently on the rope now. Less than an inch and he'd have his hand free. Free to fight and get Caleb home safe. Get home to Sadie.

Kinnard actually began to sweat. "Well, kid, ya know he wasn't goin' for our original plan. He hadn't taken you back into the house or anythin' like that. So, let's just say I got even with him for ya."

Lance fisted his hands at his sides. "I'm not going to ask you again, Jack. What did you do to my father?"

"I just slipped a little poison into his supper."

Jon struggled not to react. *Ask the question, Lance. Come on, boy, connect the dots here.* If only he could spit out the rag and yell at the boy.

"You did *what?*"

"Look, he wasn't gonna take ya back in. He's of no use to ya now. Might as well kill him and get his money." Kinnard took a cautious step backward. "I did it so ya'd git yer money, Lance."

Kinnard, scared of the kid? Jon didn't see that one coming. *Come on, Lance, ask the question. It's right there in front of your face.*

"You stupid *cooyon!* My father wrote me out of his will! If he dies now, without changing it, I get nothing! Do you understand, you fat imbecile? I get nothing!" Lance's face was redder than Jon could've ever imagined. The veins in the boy's neck were popping out at all angles.

Jon worked the rope harder. Knowing he and Caleb were being ignored for now, he wasn't as cautious about his movements.

"I—I didn't know." Kinnard took another step backward.

"You've ruined everything. First you shoot Daniels, then get the bright idea to take his picture. You wanted to blackmail my father, but that was the stupidest idea ever. Then, I fix that and get everything going smooth, you bring my parole officer out here." Lance jabbed his thumb over his shoulder, but never turned his head.

Jon worked more frantically on the rope.

Lance paid him no attention, just kept yelling and advancing on Kinnard. "Now you've gone and poisoned my father. He'll die without changing his will and I'll be destitute. You stupid moron."

"I-I'm sorry, Lance. I didn't know he'd written ya out. I'd 'a never poisoned him if I'd known."

Lance stopped advancing. His body went rigid.

Jon froze. Finally, the kid was going to ask the right question.

"How were you able to poison my father's food?"

Kinnard's ruddy face went white. No, it went whiter than white. For a moment, Jon wondered if the man would have a heart attack right on the spot.

"I asked you how you were able to poison his food."

"Well, I, uh—"

This wasn't going down a good avenue. Jon wrestled with the rope at his wrists.

"How, Jack? Tell me." Lance's body language made it perfectly clear he was barely containing his anger.

"She came to me, Lance. Said she knew what we were up to. Said she'd turn us in to the police if I didn't do what she said." Kinnard actually trembled.

Oh, no. Lance was sure to blow. Jon jerked his right hand against the rope. It caught on his thumb joint, but not tight. He made his hand as thin as possible, maneuvering the thumb and pad. Slowly, slowly…there! His hands were free.

"Who? Candy-Jo? You've been working with *her* all this time?"

Jon coughed. Neither Kinnard nor Lance spared him a glance. Jon eased his left foot over to tap Caleb.

"No, it's not like that. She caught on to what we was doin'."

Caleb glanced at Jon, who waved his free hands behind him. Caleb's eyes widened. Jon nodded, then dipped his head toward Lance and Kinnard.

Without warning, Lance reared back his fist and smacked Kinnard in the chin. The big man wavered, then slumped to the couch. Lance leaned in, right in Kinnard's face. "What kind of poison did you use? I need to know, you stupid oaf, so I can rush in and save his life. Otherwise, my life is over."

Kinnard trembled as Lance shook him. "Tell me, what poison?"

"I don't know. Rat poison."

Strychnine. Jon struggled to remember what he'd learned about the drug in his continuing education. It was a level six in toxicity rating—a small amount could kill Deacon Wynn.

"She's planned to kill him and get his money, now that I've been written out of the will." Lance straightened and checked his cell phone. "Ms. Thompson called me ten minutes ago. I don't have any idea how long it took her to call me." He glared at his partner. "How much of a dose did you use?"

"I—I don't know. A little packet."

Escape or save a life? *God, what do I do?*

Lance ran a hand over his head. "What am I going to do now?"

Save a life.

Jon pushed his hands back into position as if they were still tied and stomped his foot. Lance turned around, surprise hitting his features. In his anger, he must have totally forgotten about Jon and Caleb. "What?"

Jon stomped his foot again.

Lance crossed the room and snatched the rag from Jon's mouth. "What?"

Taking a deep breath, Jon leveled his breathing. "The poison is strychnine. It's diluted in rat poison, so you can still save his life. But the hospital needs to know what was used. They'll need to act immediately. You need to get there and tell them it was rat poison. If you wait, he could die."

Lance stood still for a moment. "But I can't get there for at least twenty minutes from here."

"Call the emergency room and tell them."

"They won't believe me. Especially if Candy-Jo's there."

Jon swallowed hard. "Then call Sadie and tell her. She'll let the hospital know and they'll trust her."

"She won't believe me. She's suspecting I'm up to something."

Jon took a deep breath. "Then let me call her."

"Are ya crazy?" Kinnard came out of his stupor, but still stayed across the room from Lance.

"Shut up, Jack. It's because of you I'm in this mess."

Jon stared at Lance. "Look, I know you're scared and you have every right to be. But we have to make that call now. Your father's life is in the balance."

Lance paused, then grabbed the Desert Eagle from Kinnard's waistband. He moved to hold the gun at Caleb's head, then opened his cell phone, dialed a number and held the phone up to Jon's ear. "Fine. You call Ms. Thompson and convince her to call the hospital. But one wrong word and she'll get to hear her brother shot. Got that?"

Oh, did he ever.

Unknown name. Unknown number.

Sadie stared at the caller ID readout. Probably a sales call, for which she so wasn't in the mood. She let it ring a second time.

"Okay to answer," the agent yelled from the living room.

Wow, she'd better call NASA—they had to be missing one of their rocket scientists. Conviction came over her instantly. That was mean and unfair. She lifted the cordless and pressed the talk button. "Hello."

"Sadie, it's Jon. Jon Garrison."

Her heart raced. As if she wouldn't recognize his voice. "Jon, where are you? I've been worried sick. I can—"

"Listen to me. I can't talk long. I need you to call the emergency room and tell them Deacon's been poisoned with strychnine, in rat poison form. They'll know what to do."

"Rat poison? How do you know about Deacon? Jon, what's going on?"

"Just do as I ask, please." Muffled sounds echoed over the line. "Time's of the essence, so you need to make the call. Will you do that for me?"

"Of course. But I—"

"The police will have questions regarding the poisoning. Have them question Candy-Jo. Seriously question her."

"O-kay. So, Lance was right? She was just after Deacon's money?"

"Yes, Lance was right. Candy-Jo is responsible for Deacon's poisoning. Now, we're fine, but you need to make that call now. Love you. Bye."

Sadie dropped the phone. It landed on the floor with a crash, the battery cover flying across the wooden floor.

"We got it. The call was made from a cellular phone registered to Lance Wynn." The FBI agent flipped open his own phone and pressed a button. "Ward, we just got a call from Jon Garrison, but on Lance Wynn's phone." He ducked back into the living room.

But Sadie didn't listen. She was shocked and numb. Jon had said he loved her.

Her heart flipped, but another part of her ached. He loved her, but did he just tell her that because he was about to die?

"Sadie, you need to call the hospital." Felicia nudged her. "The agents are working it, but you need to make sure. It could save Deacon's life."

Snapping out of her trance, Sadie bent for the phone.

"It's broken. Use mine." Felicia slipped her cell into Sadie's hands.

Sadie dialed 911, informed the operator that she had critical information needed by the emergency room personnel and asked to be patched through to the hospital. Several clicks later, and a triage nurse was on the line.

She explained about the strychnine used on Deacon. The nurse yelled out something, then hung up. Sadie ended the call, then dialed 911 again. This time when the dispatcher answered, she requested to speak to Sheriff Theriot in regard to an attempted murder. She was put on hold while the patch was activated.

Jon had said *we're fine*. Had that been his clue to her that he was with Caleb?

It had to be!

Sheriff Theriot answered in his usual rough manner. But once she told him about Jon's call, excitement filled his voice. He thanked her and hung up.

She started to close the phone, but something about Jon's voice… He *knew* Candy-Jo had poisoned Deacon. What if the sheriff just questioned her off the cuff? Sadie quickly dialed Georgia's cell phone.

She answered on the first ring. "Hello."

"Georgia, it's Sadie. How's Deacon?"

"Not so good. They've given him Valium for the spasms, but he's in a lot of pain, Candy-Jo says."

Would Valium do anything for the strychnine? "Is Candy-Jo right there near you?"

"Not right now. They let her in every so often and she stays until he has another spasm. What's going on? Have you heard from your brother?"

"In an offhand way." She was choosing to believe Jon and Caleb were together and God was keeping them safe. "Keep your voice down, in case someone can overhear you. Listen, Sheriff Theriot is going to come question Candy-Jo about Deacon being poisoned."

"Poisoned?"

"Keep your voice low, remember?"

"Okay. Poisoned?"

"Yes. I can't go into detail, right now, but he's been poisoned. And Candy-Jo's involved."

"Oh, wow. How do you know this?"

"I can't tell you, just trust me. So don't let her leave or run, okay? Do whatever it takes, but keep her there until I make sure there's physical evidence."

"Okay, you got it."

"*Merci*, Georgia. Let me know if there's any change."

Sadie returned the phone to Felicia, who fixed her another cup of hot tea. Sadie smiled her thanks and went onto the patio, reliving Jon's words again.

Her hands trembled until tea sloshed over the cup.

She rushed back inside, passing Felicia and Pastor sitting at the kitchen table, and stopped in the living room. She fisted her hands on her hips and stared at the FBI agent. "They should've found Jon by his GPS by now. What's the status?"

His eyes glazed over in a condescending way and he opened his mouth.

"No. Don't give me a runaround or patronize me. I want to know what's going on and I want to know now."

He sat up straight on the couch. "Ma'am, I can tell you they've locked on to his position and are on-site as we speak."

Her knees went weak. She eased to the arm of the chair. "They're there?"

"Yes, ma'am. I just got the information. They're surrounding the building the GPS is transmitting from."

Ice ran through Sadie's veins.

TWENTY-ONE

"You sure she'll call the hospital?" Lance grabbed his phone back from Jon, but at least he moved the gun off Caleb.

"She'll call. Probably already has." Jon wondered about the wisdom of slipping in his declaration of love, but if that was the last time he would be able to talk to her, he wanted her to know. Besides, Lance had seemed too worked up to notice.

"Think they'll listen to her?"

"Yes. She's Deacon's faithful employee and everybody in Lagniappe knows it, especially after all the media coverage. She'll make them listen."

"Good." Lance pocketed his phone and tucked the gun into his own waistband. "I hope she tells them in time."

"I'm praying he'll be fine."

Lance stopped moving. "You pray?"

Jon wrestled with the words. "I didn't for a long time, but I sure do now."

"Ya some kinda religious freak?" Kinnard dared to move closer in the room.

"What's it to you if he is?" Lance shook his head. "You know, I still can't believe you did anything Candy-Jo told you."

Kinnard moved back to his post by the door. "She was gonna tell the cops on us. I didn't have a choice."

"You always have a choice." Jon couldn't believe he'd spoken aloud. Both Lance and Kinnard stared at him. He wet his lips.

Might as well go down in flames if he had to go. "It's called free will. You can choose to do something you know is wrong or you can opt to do what's right, even if it's harder."

"Like our destiny?" Lance asked.

"No, like if you want to follow the will of God or not."

"And you listen to God?"

"I do."

"What a load of baloney." Kinnard shifted his weight from one leg to the other.

Lance directed his attention to his partner. "Just what would you know about it, Jack? I don't think you even know enough to argue."

Kinnard just grunted.

Looking back to Jon, Lance visibly relaxed his shoulders. "Do you think they'll be able to save him? That we told them in time?"

"I don't know that, son. All I know is that Sadie will make them listen to her. She's that type of woman." And his heart hurting proved how much he missed her.

"So, you're sweet on her, right?" Rats, Lance had noticed. Would he use it against Sadie, turning Jon's safety into another threat to hold over her head?

Heat warmed Jon's cheeks. "I respect and admire her, yes."

"You said you loved her on the phone." Lance glanced at Caleb. "I think he's sweet on your sister."

Jon caught movement out the screen door. He glanced at Lance and Kinnard, found them staring each other down, then looked out again.

More movement. Actually, lots of it. A lot of men in black with the reflective letters on the back of their jackets. The letters FBI.

Jon didn't think he'd ever be happy to see the men in black, but he'd been wrong.

"What are we gonna do now?" Lance asked Kinnard.

"About what?"

"My father. Them."

Jon caught Caleb's eye and nodded slightly toward the door.

Caleb wrinkled his brows. Jon nodded at the door again. Caleb followed his gaze and then his eyes went wide. He looked back at Jon.

Yes, he'd seen them. Knew what was coming.

"Maybe yer daddy will be okay."

"He'd better be or you're as good as dead."

Jon flexed his untied hands. He'd be able to help once the FBI made their move. He waved from behind his back to Caleb. The boy nodded, understanding.

"What about them? They know the whole story now."

Kinnard locked stares with Jon. "Guess they have ta go."

Lance began to pace again. "I didn't sign up for all this killing, Jack."

"We gotta protect ourselves."

Another flash of movement, this time much nearer to the door. Right at the base of the steps.

Jon glanced at the arguing men. Neither seemed aware of any movement outdoors. Jon stared at the nearest agent, begging him to look at him.

"Like you were when you teamed up with Candy-Jo?"

"I told ya, I didn't have a choice. She blackmailed me."

Jon had to smile at the irony.

Finally, the agent's gaze landed on Jon's face. Jon gave a curt nod in the direction of Lance and Kinnard. The agent held up four fingers. Four men? Uh, no. Jon shook his head.

"And you didn't bother to tell me?" Lance sat on the edge of the coffee table. Surprisingly, it held his weight. "I wonder, maybe you and Candy-Jo were in this together from the beginning, huh, Jack?"

The agent held up three fingers. Jon shook his head.

"Ya can't think that. Hey, you came to me, 'member?"

Two fingers. Jon nodded.

"Yeah, but how soon after that did you start working with Candy-Jo? Immediately?"

The agent held up the gun, then two fingers. Jon shook his head.

"I already told ya, she came to me after ya did that press release." Lance huffed.

The gun and one finger. Jon nodded.

"What would've made her think we were involved in anything from the press release?"

"I dunno, but she found me."

"Really, Jack? I find that hard to believe. There's no connection between you and me. I had to search hard to find someone with a big enough grudge to help me—someone with, well, let's just say a criminal past such as yours." Lance stood and moved toward the edge of the couch. "I don't see how she would've figured out you and I were working together. How do you suppose she did that?"

Jon eased his right hand to his side and waggled his fingers at the agent. The agent nodded.

"I didn't look for her, Lance, I swear."

"Did I say you did?" Lance took another step toward Kinnard.

"No, but sounds like that's what yer meanin'." Kinnard moved around the coffee table, almost in front of Caleb.

The agent held up five fingers.

"Seems to me that maybe our plan wasn't moving as fast as you'd like, so maybe you went looking for her. The two of you plotted to kill my father. Maybe even frame me for the murder. Is that what you planned?"

Four fingers.

"No, nothing like that."

Three fingers.

"Now why don't I believe you? Were you going to frame me for Daniels's murder? My father's, too?"

Two fingers.

"I wouldn't do that, Lance."

One finger.

"Sure you wouldn't."

The screen door burst open. "FBI, freeze!"

Lance reached for the gun in his waistband. Jon leaped off the chair, covering Caleb, and sent them both to the ground.

Shots rang out.

Jon kept his body over Caleb's head.

More shots.

He could feel Caleb trembling under him. Jon spread his arms apart on the floor to keep the bulk of his weight off the boy.

"All clear."

Slowly, Jon rolled off Caleb and sat, pulling Caleb and the chair upright.

Smoke from the guns filled the room, burning Jon's eyes. A stench coated the small area. An agent rested a gloved hand on Jon's shoulder. "Are you okay, Mr. Garrison?"

"Fine." He looked at Caleb, who had an agent untying his hands. The gag had already been removed from his mouth. Caleb coughed hard, then gave his silly, sideways grin. "I'm good."

Jon stood and stretched. A breeze drifted in, clearing the smoke.

What Jon saw nearly made him retch.

That poor FBI agent, he hadn't known what to do with her.

Sadie sped along the road toward Fisherman's Cove on the corner side of the bayou. The most isolated side in the parish. She grinned, remembering his face when she demanded to know where they were.

Oh, he'd resisted, all right. Until she'd threatened to call Lance Wynn and tell him there was a swarm of FBI agents outside his door. The poor agent had been distraught, not sure what to do. He couldn't call Ward or Lockwood because they were on the scene. He'd finally told her the location and she knew it well.

Some odd months ago, Lance had wanted his father to use that area to erect an outpost facility and let him run it. Deacon had refused him and their strained relationship had only worsened as a result.

She'd never suspected Lance to be involved in the sabotage or the blackmail, but now she had no choice but to believe that. This area. Jon's call from Lance's phone. Information about the poisoning. What was going on?

An ambulance, siren wailing, came up behind her. She eased to the side of the road. The ambulance blew by her.

Her heart pounded erratically. There wasn't anything on this road, except the old shack where Lance had taken his father that one time to pitch his idea. Which meant the rescue had already happened and someone had been hurt.

Lord, please don't let it have been Caleb or Jon. I don't think I could take that, God. Anything but losing one of them.

She pressed harder on the accelerator as her pulse throbbed. Panic and fear drove her faster, faster.

Turning onto the dirt side road, she could make out the flashing lights of the ambulance in front of her. The tires on her car squished over the road, slowing her progress. Frustration rubbed against her very being.

Sadie spied the ambulance ahead of her, under a massive live oak tree. Numerous solid navy cars parked haphazardly all over the place. She spun the steering wheel, jerking the car in behind the rescue vehicle. She slammed on the brakes, jammed the car into Park and opened the car door. Bright lights on stands washed a good quarter acre of a mile in their beams.

Not even bothering to turn off the engine, she ran toward the little shanty. Her heart rested in her throat.

"Ma'am, you can't be here."

She ignored the voice and kept moving toward the cabin. Men in black windbreakers milled all over. The paramedics carried a stretcher into the dilapidated shack.

Lord, not Caleb or Jon. Please don't take them from me.

"Sadie."

She jerked her gaze to the doorway. She rushed forward, arms wide open.

TWENTY-TWO

Beautiful, graceful, a godly woman...and here in the flesh.

Jon raced down the stairs and took her in his arms. She felt so good, like she belonged there.

"I was so worried." She lifted her face to his. Tears soaked the unblemished skin. "I didn't know where you were, or wh—"

"Shh." He kissed her temple. "I'm fine."

She jerked back. "C-Caleb?"

"Is fine. The EMTs are helping him get circulation back in his feet. He'd been sitting constantly with his feet tied in place almost since the time he'd been taken. That's a long time. He'd lost feeling."

"I need to see him."

Jon smiled. "Of course you do. Come on." He led her past the agents walking around.

Two EMTs stood on either side of the boy as they began down the steps.

"Caleb!"

The boy let go of the paramedics when he heard his name. His smile widened and he made his way slowly to her.

She rushed forward and flung her arms around him. "Oh, Caleb. I was so scared for you. Are you okay? Let me look at you."

"I'm fine, sis." Caleb chuckled and squeezed her.

"We need to ask you some questions, Mr. Garrison and Mr. Frost." Agent Ward held a notebook and pen.

"Can't it wait? Can't we go home and they come see you tomorrow?" Sadie asked.

"I'm afraid not, ma'am. We need to get their statements now, while everything's fresh in their mind. A man's been killed here today."

She gasped. "Who?"

"We aren't at liberty to disclose that information right now, ma'am."

Jon shook his head. He'd had enough of governmental red tape. So much, in fact, that he planned to resign first thing back on the job. "Lance Wynn."

"Sir." Agent Ward let out a heavy sigh.

"Oh, no." Tears filled her eyes.

"Hey, don't feel too sorry for him, sis. He kidnapped me."

She wove her arm around her brother. "I know, but he was so young. And poor Deacon...oh, this will break his heart, even though they weren't on the best of terms."

"Speaking of Deacon, how is he?" Jon asked.

Sadie shrugged. "I haven't heard since I called the hospital and told them about the poisoning."

"Why don't you call them now while we answer the agent's questions?" Jon squeezed her shoulder.

"Okay." She moved toward her car.

Jon turned to Ward. "What questions do you have?"

The agent nodded at Caleb. "First, I'd like to know how they abducted you."

Caleb turned red. "Well, Lance met me at the school as soon as classes were over. It was raining cats and dogs and he offered me a ride home so I wouldn't have to ride the bus. No one wants to be on a bus in July when it's raining and you can't let down the windows. No air-conditioning on them, you know?"

Jon leaned against the trunk of the live oak tree as the paramedics wheeled the white sheet-covered stretcher. Poor Lance, he *was* too young to die.

"And so you went with him?" Agent Ward asked.

"Yeah. I knew him from juvie, we'd hung out a couple of times since I got out, so why wouldn't I?" Caleb shook his head. "Didn't have a clue what he'd been up to."

"Then what happened?"

"Well, I noticed we weren't heading in the direction of my house pretty quick. So I asked him where he was taking me. He said he wanted to show me something really cool."

The agent scribbled furiously.

"I figured it was no big deal, so I was down with it." Caleb shrugged. "And he brought me out here. I didn't think it was so cool."

"What transpired then?"

"He showed me that tree Mr. Garrison's leaning against and asked me if I recognized it."

"Did you?"

"No. So I asked him why I would. I mean, I haven't lived in Lagniappe very long. Why would he think I would recognize it?"

"What did he say?"

"He asked didn't I recognize it from the picture they'd sent my sister."

Jon pushed off the trunk. He fought the urge to shudder. But just leaning there, being in the same place they'd taken Harold Daniels…

"And then I realized he was one of the blackmailers."

"What'd you do?"

"I went to slug him, of course. And that's when he pulled the gun." Caleb lifted a single shoulder. "He ordered me inside, tied me up, and there I sat until you guys showed up."

Jon snapped his head up. "Wait a minute. Caleb, what gun did Lance pull on you?"

"The one he used in the shoot-out with the FBI agents."

"That gun wasn't his. That Desert Eagle is the one Kinnard brought with him."

"Well, he had one because he pulled it on me."

Agent Ward turned and yelled for his partner to come over.

"Did we recover any gun but the Desert Eagle from Lance Wynn's body?"

"No, just that one. Why?"

Jon glanced at Agent Ward. "So where's the other gun?"

"Thanks, Georgia." Sadie hung up the phone and looked over the area ablaze with all the lights standing everywhere. Agent Ward talked with Jon and Caleb under the big tree.

The ambulance maneuvered around her car, lights on but no siren. On their way to the morgue, no doubt. A twinge of guilt rested on Sadie. Why hadn't she sensed Lance's involvement in all of this? Maybe she could have prevented this entire tragedy.

Several cars had doors open, radios squealing from inside. Men milled about, carrying little envelopes. A couple stood next to a car or two. An occasional chuckle rose up into the air. A breeze came off the bayou, carrying the hint of fish on its wings.

One car sat off by itself, near the shack. A single silhouette darkened the interior—Jack Kinnard.

She glanced around again. Ward was busy. Most of the others moving around were either too busy or wouldn't give her the time of day. Maybe no one would notice her approach. She wanted to know *why*. Why he'd done all this. What he'd hoped to accomplish. How could it possibly have been worth two men losing their lives?

No one said a word as she picked her way around the mess to the car. Not even the cop on watch. She walked alongside the cruiser. The back windows were down against the July heat.

"Well, hello there, Ms. Thompson."

Sadie's mouth went dry. "Mr. Kinnard, I presume?"

"You should know me well."

Her skin crawled just being in such close proximity to the man. Never before had she felt evil radiating so strongly from someone. But she squared her shoulders and looked him straight in the eye. "Why would you do this?"

"Deacon Wynn ain't nothing but a money-hungry man. He sold us workers out fer what? To make more money for hisself."

"He was upgrading, Mr. Kinnard. What most businesses do."

"That wasn't it. He didn't want to pay us no more. Keep all those profits to hisself, that's what he did. He deserves to die."

The heartlessness of the man chilled Sadie's heart. "Then you'll be disappointed to know that the hospital doctors were able to treat Mr. Wynn's poisoning. He's resting comfortably now."

Pure hatred blinked in his eyes.

"Oh, and Sheriff Theriot has taken Mrs. Wynn into custody for accessory to attempted murder."

Fear mixed into his expression.

"Oh, yes, she's named you her accomplice. Said you came to her with the idea to kill Deacon and blame it all on Lance."

He dropped his head in a dejected manner.

"If I were you, Mr. Kinnard, I'd start thinking of a good defense attorney. You're going to need one."

"Ma'am, you shouldn't be over here. This is restricted." The agent nodded toward Mr. Kinnard. "He's been arrested. You can't talk to him."

"I've said all I need to anyway."

The agent gave her a funny look, but she ignored him.

"Hey, you, I gotta go to the bathroom now or I'm gonna make a mess in yer car."

Sadie shook her head at the man's audacity.

The car door squeaked behind her. "Stay over here, by the steps where I can see you," the agent ordered.

"I need my hands, buddy." Kinnard didn't sound one bit fazed by his situation.

She stopped, not wanting to head to the tree where Jon and Caleb still stood, answering Agent Ward's questions. Heaven forbid she should interrupt.

She could go back to her car, but she didn't want to get too far away from Jon and Caleb—not after having nearly lost them both today. Sadie smiled. Jon had said he loved her on the phone. Once she got him away from this place, she'd grill him about that.

"What th— Freeze!"

She turned toward the sound of the yell and was nearly knocked off her feet. Jack Kinnard gripped her from the side, a gun pressed to her temple. "Back off, everybody. Back off or she takes a bullet to the brain."

Ice shot through Jon's veins.

"Kinnard. He has a gun. And Sadie." He rushed forward, only to have Agent Ward grip his arm tightly.

"Let us handle this, Garrison."

"But it's Sadie. How'd he get a gun?"

"Must've had it stashed. Whichever moron let him outta cuffs will pay later. You stay here." Ward had already unholstered his weapon, as had all the other agents on the grounds. He lifted the radio mic on his Kevlar vest. "I want to know where and how he got that gun and I want to know now."

Caleb moved next to Jon. "We have to save her."

"Shh."

Ward's radio came to life, but in low tones. "He must've had the gun hidden under the stairs. He was taken out of the car to go to the bathroom and got it then."

Ward shook his head. He pointed at Jon and Caleb, mouthed the word *stay*, then moved forward to join the other agents advancing on Kinnard.

"Give it up, Kinnard. You're in enough trouble as it is." Agent Lockwood crept down the stairs toward them. "You've got nowhere to go. Put down the gun."

"Ya ain't takin' me in." Kinnard moved backward, pulling Sadie with him. Tears glistened on her face, reflected off the lights.

Jon fisted his hands. He surveyed the area. Kinnard had to be taking Sadie to her car. It was the only possible escape route for him. "Wait here," he told Caleb, then crouched and headed toward Sadie's car.

"Just let go of Ms. Thompson. Nobody else needs to get hurt."

Sadie's muffled sobs nearly tore Jon's heart from his chest. He'd make sure Kinnard didn't hurt her. Finally, he made it to her car. As quietly as possible, he eased open the back door and slipped inside. He shut it with barely a click.

The lights weren't pointed in this direction. Darkness was his cover as he crouched on the backseat floorboard behind the passenger seat. If he'd guessed correctly, Kinnard would enter through the passenger door, shove Sadie behind the driver's seat and sit in the center.

The perfect location for Jon to grab him from behind and get the gun away.

"Don't come any closer or she dies. I mean it." Kinnard's voice was loud, right outside the car.

God, please give me the strength and courage to do this and not get Sadie hurt.

"Back off, I tell ya."

The passenger door opened. The interior light brightened the car. Jon held his breath, praying Kinnard wouldn't think to look in the backseat. Kinnard shoved Sadie into the car, pushing her behind the steering wheel. He closed the passenger-side door. Darkness returned to sit over the car's cabin.

"Please, just take my car. Let me go."

"Oh, no, Ms. High and Mighty. You and me, we're going fer a ride. Maybe have a little fun. Ya've sure caused me enough sufferin'."

Jon's muscles tensed. Sadie sobbed.

"Shut up. Start the car."

Where were the agents? Were they about to make their move? Jon would hate to pop up and accidentally get shot.

"Let my sister go."

What was Caleb doing? Jon sent him silent messages to be quiet, not to try and be a hero—ignoring his own conscience that reminded him he was doing that exact thing.

"Start the car."

Sadie whimpered, but the car's engine hummed to life.

"Good, now put it in gear and let's get outta here."

The car jerked.

"No."

The brake engaged, nearly rolling Jon into the backs of the front seats.

"Don't back up. Just drive around these morons."

The gearshift popped.

Now or never.

Jon jumped, bringing his right arm to tighten around Kinnard's neck. His left hand grabbed the gun, but Kinnard didn't let it go.

"Get out," Jon growled at Sadie.

She killed the ignition and, taking the keys with her, opened the door. "Help Jon. He's got Kinnard," she yelled as she slipped out, leaving the door wide. Light flooded the car.

Jon struggled to get control of the gun. Kinnard was strong, very strong. All four doors opened, and agents swarmed. Yeah, twice the feds had showed up just in the nick of time. Jon let go of his hold on Kinnard.

A gunshot erupted.

Kinnard was thrown out of the car, covered by agents yelling.

Jon's left shoulder burned. Must've jammed it during his wrestling match with the bigger man. He reached to rub it. His hand came away wet. And red.

Sadie rushed to the backseat. "Oh, somebody help. Jon's been shot."

TWENTY-THREE

Surprisingly, being shot didn't hurt nearly as bad as everyone made it out.

Jon shifted against the vinyl backseat of Ward and Lockwood's car. It would've taken a good twenty minutes for another ambulance to arrive, so the agents had graciously volunteered to rush him to the hospital in their car. He just might have to change his opinion of the federal boys yet.

The siren and lights were activated, but Jon kept telling them there was no need. He wasn't in a lot of pain and he kept the folded undershirt—donated by none other than Ward—tight against the wound. He did like sitting between Caleb and Sadie and having her fuss over him. It was nice, for a change, to be the center of attention. In a good sort of way.

"Are you okay?" she whispered.

"Fine." He patted her hand. So sweet that worry lined her beautiful wide eyes as she stared at him.

Kinnard had been apprehended, of course, and was en route to the sheriff's office now for booking. Didn't look good for him—charges would include murder, sabotage, aiding and abetting in kidnapping, kidnapping and attempted murder of an officer of the court. No way would he be offered a plea agreement.

"Does it hurt much?" Caleb asked.

"Not really. Stings. Like I got stung by a really mad bee."

Caleb chuckled. The boy would be okay. Jon had been wrong about him. So wrong. And he'd been wrong about Sadie. He also hadn't seen Lance's involvement with every-thing until it was too late. Somewhere down the line, his judgment had become skewed. It was time to get out of his line of work.

A month ago, had he come to this realization, he'd be packing it up, heading back to Nebraska. Now…well, he and Sadie had a lot to talk about. But he couldn't imagine going on without her in his life. As much as he detested the bayou, if this was where Sadie wanted to stay, then stay here he would. If she wanted him to stay.

Sadie tightened her grip on his right hand. Could she know what he was thinking? She smiled and snuggled closer to him. With everything that had happened, maybe she'd want to get out of Lagniappe. Out of Louisiana, period.

"Here we are." Agent Lockwood brought the car to a halt right outside the emergency room.

Agent Ward jumped out of the car and opened the back door. Sadie eased out, then helped Jon. Caleb walked around from the other side of the car.

"I'll park and be right in," Lockwood said as he slipped the car in gear.

Ward entered through the automatic doors first, barking orders at the nurses to get a doctor ready pronto. Jon smiled. Yeah, he might even grow to like these feds.

He made it to the counter before dizziness washed over him. He swayed, but Sadie shoved a wheelchair under him in time to catch him. He smiled his gratitude. He felt a little woozy, a little lightheaded all of a sudden.

The nurse wheeled him down the hall, admonishing Sadie and Caleb to go to the waiting room. He held up his right fingers, waggling them.

And then the room spun until all he could sense was warm darkness.

* * *

"He's doing great. Doctors said he should be fine, with no permanent damage." Georgia handed Sadie a cup of coffee.

"What?"

"Deacon. He's gonna be just fine. Isn't that why you're here? To check up on him?" Her assistant smiled. "I saw your brother at the soda machine when I was getting your coffee. Guess that all worked out okay, too, huh?"

"Actually I'm here because Jon was shot."

"Jon?" Georgia scrunched her brows.

"Jon Garrison. Caleb's parole officer."

"Oh. Right. The guy at the office."

Sadie smiled despite herself. "Yes. That's him."

"Shot?" Georgia dropped to the seat beside Sadie. "You gotta fill me in, girl."

"It's a long story." She took a sip of the coffee, then shivered. Hospital coffee had to be the worst. But bad coffee was better than no coffee. Especially if she was to stay awake this time of the night.

"I've got the time. I want to hear it."

Sadie filled her assistant in on what all had transpired. And it was amusing—she'd never noticed how animated Georgia's face was. When she was done, Georgia put her arm around Sadie's shoulders. "Girl, you've had a day to end all days."

Wasn't that the truth? "It's been one of the worst, but one of the best, too."

Georgia wrinkled her nose. "I get the worst, but how do you figure the best?"

Sadie laughed. "Because I realized just how good God is, how much I really love my brother and how much Jon Garrison means to me."

"Ah. I see." Georgia gave her a sideways hug, then dropped her hand. She cleared her throat. "Looks like your brother's heading this way. Why don't I go track down a nurse and see how Deacon's doing? Give y'all a little time alone."

"*Merci.*"

Georgia patted Caleb's shoulder as she passed him in the hall. He gave her a funny look, then plopped down in the chair beside Sadie. "Wonder how long it'll be before they come out and tell us anything."

She glanced to the other side of the waiting room, where Ward and Lockwood sat thumbing through some outdated magazines. "I'm sure they know the FBI is out here waiting, so maybe it won't take too long."

"Hope so." He took a long draw off his canned soda.

She pinched the bridge of her nose. "You know, Caleb, it sounds like you're worried about him."

Her brother jerked his head up, staring at the ceiling. "I care about the dude." He made eye contact with her and smiled. "Don't get me wrong, I didn't want to even like him. But he's cool. A good guy."

"I think so, too."

"You know, I was sitting there when he called you. When Lance made him call."

And he'd heard what Jon had said. Heat fanned against her face.

"It's okay, you know. You two hooking up. I'm cool with that."

Relief chased the happiness in her heart. "I'm glad. Caleb, I know you've been here only for a short time, but I have to tell you, I can't imagine my life without you in it." Her voice cracked.

His face turned as red as the soda can in his hand. He let out a throat-clearing sound. "Me, too."

That was about as close as she'd get to a declaration of love from him and it was enough for her. She smiled and hugged her brother. "I do love you, Caleb, and I'm so glad you're here with me."

"Yeah, me, too."

A nurse interrupted the moment. "Who's with Jon Garrison?"

Sadie and Caleb shoved to their feet, as did the two FBI agents. The four of them crowded around the nurse. She flustered for a moment before composing herself. "The bullet went straight through, so no surgery is required."

"How's he doing?" Ward demanded.

"We're closing the wound now. He lost a good bit of blood, so we're giving him a transfusion. As soon as that's complete, we'll make sure he has pain medication."

"When can I see him?" Sadie wanted nothing more than to just look at him, see for herself that he really was okay.

"The transfusion will be complete in about an hour. His wound should be dressed within that time, as well."

"So, in about an hour we can see him?"

"It depends on how well he does with the transfusion. Right now, he's in and out of consciousness."

"Is that common?" Lockwood asked.

"Very common with blood loss such as Mr. Garrison sustained. Not to worry, we're monitoring his blood pressure and vitals."

"But he'll be okay, yes?" Sadie held her breath for the answer.

"The doctor doesn't anticipate any complications at this point."

Sadie let out her breath. *Thank You, Jesus.*

If this was heaven, he wanted to stay.

Bright lights shone down on him, but Jon didn't feel the need to squint. Everything was hazy anyway. He was warm and felt like he was floating. Cocooned, that's what he felt like.

"Jon. Jon."

He turned his head to the right. Wow, Sadie was in heaven, too? Nah, must mean he was dreaming. Oh, what a dream. He smiled, feeling little bubbles of happiness dancing in his stomach. "Hey, Sadie."

Her laughter echoed in his mind. Dreams were so nice. "I love you, Sadie. You're so beautiful."

More of her laughter tinkled inside his head. "You're out of it because of the pain medication."

"Nope. Not so. You are beautiful and I do love you."

"We'll talk about that when you're fully conscious of what you're saying."

"Let's run away together."

Her laughter filled him with such happiness. "To where?"

"Nebraska. I didn't sell my place there. We could take Caleb and move there."

"What about your job?"

"I'm gonna quit anyway. I've lost per-cep-tion." His tongue had grown to double its regular size, and his mouth was stuffed with cotton.

She laughed again. He felt her hand on his forearm. "You just rest now, we'll talk about this later."

He could feel her touch. What a detailed dream.

Jon turned his attention back to the bright lights. Warm and comforting.

He loved dreamland.

TWENTY-FOUR

Had Jon's subconscious been speaking while his pain medications held his conscious in check?

Sadie watched Jon move in and out of sleep all night. His words had warmed her heart. But when he woke up, would he still say the same thing? He'd been talking some nonsense—quitting his job and running away back to Nebraska. Maybe it'd all been just that, nonsense talk.

But, oh, she wished he really did feel that way.

She'd gone up and seen Deacon earlier when they'd moved Jon into a room for overnight observation. Deacon had been devastated to learn about Lance's death and his involvement in the sabotages and blackmail against Sadie. He was just as crushed to learn of Candy-Jo's intent to kill him for his money. She didn't blame him one bit when he told her he was going to sell Vermilion Oil as soon as he could. New management might mean she'd be out of a job, but she understood how he felt.

Seemed like everyone had been touched by the evil spent over the bayou by greed and deception.

Agents Ward and Lockwood had been kind enough to escort Caleb home. She hadn't wanted him to be alone, so Pastor had agreed to crash on the couch for what was left of the night.

Now, as the sun crested over Lagniappe, its rays tossing out promise and hope, Sadie returned her attention to Jon.

*Father, thank You so much for keeping him and Caleb safe.
And for touching our hearts for one another. I really have fallen
for him, God.*

"Sadie?"

She opened her eyes and lifted her head to find Jon staring at
her. "Hi, there." She moved to the chair beside his bed, stretching a bit as she crossed the short space. "How're you feeling?"

"Okay, I think." He shifted the pillows behind him. "You're
really here now, right?"

She smiled. "Yep."

"I had some amazing dreams. You were in them."

"Was I now?"

"Yes." He grinned, warming her all over.

"Uh, Jon, you were on pain medication, in and out of consciousness."

His smile slipped off his face. "And you were here?"

"Yes."

Pink teased his cheeks. "It wasn't a dream, was it?"

"Afraid not." Did he want to pretend it was just a dream, that
he hadn't said all these wonderful things? She pinched the bridge
of her nose.

He sat, tugging the sheet up under his arms. "And you heard
everything I said?"

She pressed her lips together and nodded. *Please don't say
you didn't mean any of it.* She couldn't take that.

"Huh." He licked his lips and stared her dead in the eye.
"Well, guess you should know that I meant every crazy word of
it."

Her heart would explode at any given moment. "Jon, you
were on heavy pain medication."

"You think that made me lie?"

"No. I just—"

"Give me your hand."

She put her trembling one in his. She could feel his strength
from just that touch.

"I told you I loved you on the phone, too."

Oh, no. She could feel the tears creeping up her throat to clog her eyes. "I didn't think you meant it."

"I meant it more than you could know. If that was the last time I talked to you, I wanted you to know how I felt."

Boogers! The tears made it up into her eyes. "I—I—"

"I love you, Sadie Thompson."

"And I love you."

He smiled wider than she'd ever seen. "Then lean down here and give me a kiss before I go crazy."

What a beautiful day in the bayou!

Everything looked greener, fresher to Jon. Or maybe it was the security of being in love with someone that made such an impression. Either way, happiness rode on his back as he sat on his porch, waiting for Sadie to arrive.

She'd been adamant about bringing over lunch for them to share. He could really get used to such a situation.

Nerves attacked him as her car pulled into the driveway. He had so much to tell her, so much to ask…he'd been praying all morning that she'd be receptive to him and his ideas. The moment of truth had arrived.

He moved down the stairs and met her at the car. He planted a quick peck on her lips as she smiled up at him. Together, they carried paper sacks into his kitchen as she prattled about Caleb and wondering what she was going to do now that Mr. Wynn had sold the oil company to a bigger one, which already had a public relations team in place.

Thank You, God, for putting things in place for her to be receptive to my suggestions. Help me word my ideas in a non-offensive way.

They sat at the table, plates in front of them, and prayed together. Jon's heart lurched. Who would've ever thought he'd be sitting with a woman he loved, holding her hand and praying with her? He'd never felt so blessed.

He felt the nudge to broach the subject with her as he took a bite of the delicious yet spicy crawfish pie. He swallowed. "So, have you thought about what you're going to do now that you're out of a job?"

"Gee, thanks for rubbing it in." But she smiled. "I really don't know yet. I hadn't thought about it."

"You know, Nebraska has some really large companies that are always looking to hire good PR folks."

"Nebraska?"

"Yeah. I still have my place there. I'm thinking about maybe moving back there." He took a sip of water, studying her over the rim.

Her face went pale. "But your job is here."

"I was serious about quitting. I've already typed my letter of resignation. In two weeks, I'm officially unemployed."

"Oh." Her lips stayed in an O shape.

This wasn't going the way he'd planned. He set down his fork and reached for her hand. "I'm doing this all wrong. I've quit my job because I don't enjoy it anymore. It's time for me to move on to something different. I was thinking of working with teens in a halfway house or something."

"That's a great idea, Jon." Her eyes lit up, but her face was still pale.

"And I have connections in Nebraska. I could get something started up there and I already have a place."

Her eyes filled with moisture. "I think that's a wonderful idea."

"So, what do you say?"

"I don't know what you mean. I think it sounds lovely and if that's what you want to do, you should pursue it."

He squeezed her hand. "You still don't get it. I'm asking you to go with me. Caleb, too."

"What? But my home is here."

"But you no longer have a job and you've said before that Lagniappe hasn't been the nicest to you."

"But what about Caleb?"

"Why don't you ask him? He's not from Lagniappe. Maybe he'd like a fresh start, too. Away from everything."

"I don't know." Uncertainty hovered in her eyes.

"Think about it, pray about it." Please, please say yes.

"But I can't just up and run off with you, Jon. It wouldn't be right."

Oh, he'd really messed this all up royally. He laughed as he pushed back his chair. He kneeled on the floor beside her and took her hand. "Here, let me try again. I love you, Sadie. I know it's soon, but I know my feelings are real. And I would love nothing more than for you to agree to be my life partner. To share my heart, body, dreams and life with. Will you do me the honor of being my wife?"

EPILOGUE

Three weeks later

"You ready?" Sadie smiled at her brother.

He slung his duffel over his shoulder. "Yep, all ready."

"Head on out to the moving truck, then. I'll lock up."

Alone, Sadie did a final walk-through of her house. Well, it wasn't hers anymore. Mike Fontenot and his fiancée, Jon's former assistant, Lisa, had bought the house and would move in right after their wedding in two weeks.

But that didn't stop the memories from flooding her. The bathroom tile she'd saved up three months to have laid. The wallpaper in the living room that she'd hung herself. So much of her life over the past four years sat in this house.

The horn honked outside.

She smiled and turned to the front door. Saying goodbye to the house wasn't as hard when she had a wedding band on her finger, a brother excited about seeing a different part of the States and a husband who loved her unconditionally.

Sadie locked the front door for the last time, slipped the key under the welcome mat and smiled up toward heaven.

Thank You, Father, for so many blessings. May this house bring Mike and Lisa much joy.

The horn honked again. This time, Jon and Caleb waved at her from the cabin of the moving truck.

"Come on, sis. Daylight's wasting."

She bounced down the steps, ready for a new adventure. One filled with love…and hope.

And Jon and Caleb.

What more could she ever want? Father had read her heart and given her the dreams of her soul.

Amen.

* * * * *

Dear Reader,

Thank you for journeying with me through the Louisiana bayou as I've shared with you the characters from Lagniappe. It is bittersweet that this is the last installment of the bayou series. I've grown to feel like these characters are friends of mine and I'll miss visiting with them every day.

The stories in this series are all very near and dear to my heart. Some of the spiritual lessons the characters have learned are mine and some are shared by family very close to me. Throughout these six books, I've laughed and cried. I hope that each story has touched your heart in some small way.

I love hearing from readers. Please visit me at:

www.robincaroll.com

and drop me a line, or write to me at PO Box 242091, Little Rock, AR 72223. I invite you to join my newsletter group and sign my guestbook. I look forward to hearing from you. After reading one of my books, if you've felt led to give your life to Christ, please contact me immediately so I may send you a special gift.

Blessings,

Robin Caroll

QUESTIONS FOR DISCUSSION

1. Sadie has a past reputation that kept haunting her. How has a past reputation of yours, good or bad, affected your life now?

2. Jon feels very out of his element in Louisiana, having moved from Nebraska. Have you ever felt like that? How did you deal with the situation?

3. Caleb comes into Sadie's life at a difficult time and doesn't ease her worries in the beginning. Have you ever felt burdened by a family member? How did you deal with the emotions?

4. Jon has become cynical and judgmental after years on his job. Have you ever found yourself being or thinking judgmentally? How did you reconcile your thoughts?

5. Sadie's position at work constantly puts her in the public eye, even though she'd prefer not to be so that she could live down her past. Have you ever been put in such a situation? How did you handle it?

6. Jon has allowed another person to have great impact on his own faith. Have you ever had someone influence your beliefs? Explain.

7. Caleb is basically a good kid who's done something foolish and paid the consequences. How do you feel about rehabilitation and punishment? Why?

8. Deacon Wynn's son goes to extremes because of his greed, yet, in the end, he's right about his father's wife. In his

case, do you feel like the end justified the means? Why or why not?

9. Sadie feels alone quite a bit due to her past. Have you ever been overwhelmed with loneliness? What did you do?

10. Jon has to learn to let go of his painful past to move on to love again. How has your past affected you? What have you done to overcome past influences and move on to the future?

11. Caleb is thrust into a new town and a very strained situation. At first, he acts out in typical teenage attitude, but then he softens toward his sister. Have you ever had a family member who was difficult because of his/her personal situation? How did you react?

12. Sadie is put in a difficult situation by the blackmailers. Have you ever felt like you were "between a rock and a hard place" where neither option was good for you? What did you do?

13. Jack Kinnard is bitter because he's been laid off due to new technology. Have you ever lost a job? How did that make you feel? How did you cope?

14. Even during trying times and trials we don't understand, God is our protector. How can you back up that statement with Scripture?

15. Sadie and Jon have to learn to trust one another. Have you ever found it difficult to trust someone? How did you handle the emotions and the situation?

When a tornado strikes a small Kansas town, Maya Logan sees a new, tender side of her serious boss. Could a family man be lurking beneath Greg Garrison's gruff exterior?

Turn the page for a sneak preview of their story in
HEALING THE BOSS'S HEART
by Valerie Hansen,
Book 1 in the new six-book
AFTER THE STORM miniseries
available beginning July 2009 from Love Inspired®.

Maya Logan had been watching the skies with growing concern and already had her car keys in hand when she jerked open the door to the office to admit her boss. He held a young boy in his arms. "Get inside. Quick!"

Gregory Garrison thrust the squirming child at her. "Here. Take him. I'm going back after his dog. He refused to come in out of the storm without Charlie."

"Don't be ridiculous." She clutched his arm and pointed. "You'll never catch him. Look." Tommy's dog had taken off running the minute the hail had started.

Debris was swirling through the air in ever-increasing amounts and the hail had begun to pile in lumpy drifts along the curb. It had flattened the flowers she'd so lovingly placed in the planters and buried their stubbly remnants under inches of white, icy crystals.

In the distance, the dog had its tail between its legs and was disappearing into the maelstrom. Unless the frightened animal responded to commands to return, there was no chance of anyone catching up to it.

Gregory took a deep breath and hollered, "Char-lie," but Maya could tell he was wasting his breath. The soggy mongrel didn't even slow.

"Take the boy and head for the basement," Gregory yelled at

her. Ducking inside, he had to put his shoulder to the heavy door and use his full weight to close and latch it.

She shoved Tommy back at him. "No. I have to go get Layla."

"In this weather? Don't be an idiot."

"She's my daughter. She's only three. She'll be scared to death if I'm not there."

"She's in the preschool at the church, right? They'll take care of the kids."

"No. I'm going after her."

"Use your head. You can't help Layla if you get yourself killed." He grasped her wrist, holding tight.

Maya struggled, twisting her arm till it hurt. "Let me go. I'm going to my baby. She's all I've got."

"That's crazy! A tornado is coming. If the hail doesn't knock you out cold, the tornado's likely to bury you."

"I don't care."

"Yes, you do."

"No, I don't! Let go of me." To her amazement, he held fast. No one, especially a man, was going to treat her this way and get away with it. No one.

"Stop. Think," he shouted, staring at her as if she were deranged.

She continued to struggle, to refuse to give in to his will, his greater strength. "No. *You* think. I'm going to my little girl. That's all there is to it."

"How? Driving?" He indicated the street, which now looked distorted due to the vibrations of the front window. "It's too late. Look at those cars. Your head isn't half as hard as that metal is and it's already full of dents."

"But…"

She knew in her mind that he was right, yet her heart kept insisting she must do something. Anything. *Please, God, help me. Tell me what to do!*

Her heart was still pounding, her breath shallow and rapid, yet part of her seemed to suddenly accept that her boss was right. That couldn't be. She belonged with Layla. She was her mother.

"We're going to take shelter," Gregory ordered, giving her arm a tug. "Now."

That strong command was enough to renew Maya's resolve and wipe away the calm assurances she had so briefly embraced. She didn't go easily or quietly. Screeching, "No, no, no," she dragged her feet, stumbling along as he pulled and half dragged her toward the basement access.

Staring into the storm moments ago, she had felt as if the fury of the weather was sucking her into a bottomless black hole. Her emotions were still trapped in those murky, imaginary depths, still floundering, sinking, spinning out of control. She pictured Layla, with her silky, long dark hair and beautiful brown eyes.

"If anything happens to my daughter I'll never forgive you!" she screamed at him.

"I'll take my chances."

Maya knew without a doubt that she'd meant exactly what she'd said. If her precious little girl was hurt she'd never forgive herself for not trying to reach her. To protect her. And she'd never forgive Gregory Garrison for preventing her from making the attempt. *Never.*

She had to blink to adjust to the dimness of the basement as he shoved her in front of him and forced her down the wooden stairs.

She gasped, coughed. The place smelled musty and sour, totally in character with the advanced age of the building. How long could that bank of brick and stone stores and offices stand against a storm like this? If these walls ever started to topple, nothing would stop their total collapse. Then it wouldn't matter whether they were outside or down here. They'd be just as dead.

That realization sapped her strength and left her almost without sensation. When her boss let go of her wrist and slipped his arm around her shoulders to guide her into a corner next to an abandoned elevator shaft, she was too emotionally numb to continue to fight him. All she could do was pray and continue to repeat, "Layla, Layla," over and over again.

"We'll wait it out here," he said. "This has to be the strongest part of the building."

Maya didn't believe a word he said.

Tommy's quiet sobbing, coupled with her soul-deep concern for her little girl, brought tears to her eyes. She blinked them back, hoping she could control her emotions enough to fool the boy into believing they were all going to come through the tornado unhurt.

As for her, she wasn't sure. Not even the tiniest bit.

All she could think about was her daughter. *Dear Lord, are You watching out for Layla? Please, please, please! Take care of my precious little girl.*

* * * * *

See the rest of Maya and Greg's story when
HEALING THE BOSS'S HEART
hits the shelves in July 2009.
And be sure to look for all six of the books in the
AFTER THE STORM series, where you can follow
the residents of High Plains, Kansas,
as they rebuild their town—and find love in the process.

Maya Logan has always thought of her boss, Greg Garrison, as a hard-nosed type of guy. But when a tornado strikes their small Kansas town, Greg is quick to help however he can, including rebuilding her home. Maya soon discovers that he's building a home for them to share.

Look for

Healing the Boss's Heart

by

Valerie Hansen

Available July
wherever books are sold.

Steeple
Hill®

LI87536

REQUEST YOUR FREE BOOKS!
2 FREE RIVETING INSPIRATIONAL NOVELS
PLUS 2 FREE MYSTERY GIFTS

YES! Please send me 2 FREE Love Inspired® Suspense novels and my 2 FREE mystery gifts (gifts are worth about $10). After receiving them, if I don't wish to receive any more books, I can return the shipping statement marked "cancel". If I don't cancel, I will receive 4 brand-new novels every month and be billed just $4.24 per book in the U.S. or $4.74 per book in Canada. That's a savings of over 20% off the cover price. It's quite a bargain! Shipping and handling is just 50¢ per book.* I understand that accepting the 2 free books and gifts places me under no obligation to buy anything. I can always return a shipment and cancel at any time. Even if I never buy another book, the two free books and gifts are mine to keep forever.

123 IDN EYM2 323 IDN EYNE

Name _____ (PLEASE PRINT) _____

Address _____ Apt. # _____

City _____ State/Prov. _____ Zip/Postal Code _____

Signature (if under 18, a parent or guardian must sign)

Mail to Steeple Hill Reader Service:
IN U.S.A.: P.O. Box 1867, Buffalo, NY 14240-1867
IN CANADA: P.O. Box 609, Fort Erie, Ontario L2A 5X3

Not valid to current subscribers of Love Inspired Suspense books.

Want to try two free books from another series?
Call 1-800-873-8635 or visit www.morefreebooks.com

* Terms and prices subject to change without notice. Prices do not include applicable taxes. Sales tax applicable in N.Y. Canadian residents will be charged applicable provincial taxes and GST. Offer not valid in Quebec. This offer is limited to one order per household. All orders subject to approval. Credit or debit balances in a customer's account(s) may be offset by any other outstanding balance owed by or to the customer. Please allow 4 to 6 weeks for delivery. Offer available while quantities last.

Your Privacy: Steeple Hill Books is committed to protecting your privacy. Our Privacy Policy is available online at www.SteepleHill.com or upon request from the Reader Service. From time to time we make our lists of customers available to reputable third parties who may have a product or service of interest to you. If you would prefer we not share your name and address, please check here. ☐

LISUS09

HEARTWARMING INSPIRATIONAL ROMANCE

Experience stories
centered on love and faith
with a variety of romances
just for you,
with 10 books every month!

Love Inspired®:
Enjoy four contemporary,
heartwarming romances every month.

Love Inspired® Historical:
Travel to a different time with two powerful
and engaging stories of romance, adventure
and faith every month.

Love Inspired® Suspense:
Enjoy four contemporary tales of intrigue
and romance every month.

Steeple
Hill®

*Available every month wherever books are
sold, including most bookstores, supermarkets,
drugstores and discount stores.*

Love Inspired
SUSPENSE

TITLES AVAILABLE NEXT MONTH

Available July 14, 2009

WITNESS TO MURDER by Jill Elizabeth Nelson

Poised for an interview, TV reporter Hallie Berglund walks
into a murder scene instead. She wants the killer brought to
justice—but has she identified the right man? Her colleague
Brody Jordan knows Hallie can find the truth...if she's willing
to unearth the secrets of the past.

SOMEONE TO TRUST by Ginny Aiken

Carolina Justice

So what if she's the fire chief's daughter? Arson investigator
Rand Mason knows too much about Catelyn Caldwell's past
to trust her. Yet Cate's not the girl he remembers. And
when she needs Rand's help, it's time to see if she's become
someone he can believe in—and love.

DEADLY INTENT by Camy Tang

The Grant family's Sonoma spa is a place for rest and
relaxation—not murder! Then Naomi Grant finds her client
bleeding to death, and everything falls apart. Naomi's
reputation and freedom are at stake, and her only solace
is with the *other* suspect, Dr. Devon Knightley, the victim's
ex-husband. But he's hiding something from Naomi....

THE KIDNAPPING OF KENZIE THORN by Liz Johnson

Myles Parsons is just another inmate in Kenzie Thorn's GED
course—until he kidnaps her and reveals the truth. He's
Myles Borden, FBI agent, undercover because someone
wants her dead. But he promises he'll keep her safe. His
heart won't accept anything else.

LISCNMBPA0609